T0145516

Daughters of Nijo

A Romance of Japan

Daughters of Nijo

A Romance of Japan

Onoto Watanna

MINT EDITIONS

Daughters of Nijo: A Romance of Japan was first published in 1904.

This edition published by Mint Editions 2021.

ISBN 9781513271316 | E-ISBN 9781513276311

Published by Mint Editions®

 MINT
EDITIONS

minteditionbooks.com

Publishing Director: Jennifer Newens
Design & Production: Rachel Lopez Metzger
Project Manager: Micaela Clark
Typesetting: Westchester Publishing Services

Contents

Before the Story's Action

In the early part of the year of the Restoration there lived within the Province of Echizen a young farmer named Yamada Kwacho. Although he belonged only to the agricultural class, he was known and honored throughout the entire province, for at one time he had saved the life of the Daimio of the province, the powerful Lord of Echizen, premier to the shogunate.

In spite of the favor of the Daimio of the province, Yamada Kwacho made no effort to rise above the class to which he had been born. Satisfied with his estate, he was proud of his simple and honest calling. So the Lord of Echizen, having no opportunity of repaying the young farmer for his service, contented himself perforce with a promise that if at any time Yamada Kwacho should require his aid, he would not fail him.

Kwacho, therefore, lived happily in the knowledge of his prince's favor; and since he possessed an excellent little farm which yielded him a comfortable living, he had few cares.

He had reached the age of twenty-five years before he began to cast about him for a wife. Because of his renown in the province, Kwacho might have chosen a maiden of much higher rank than his own; but, being of a sensible mind and nature, he sought a bride within his own class. He found her in the person of little Ohano, the daughter of a neighboring farmer. She was as plump, rosy, and pretty as is possible for a Japanese maiden. Moreover, she was docile and gentle by temperament, and had all the admirable domestic virtues attractive to the eye of a youth of the character of Yamada Kwacho.

Though their courtship was brief, their wedding was splendid, for the Prince of Echizen himself bestowed upon them gifts with all good wishes and congratulations. Life seemed to bear a more joyous aspect to Kwacho. He went about his work whistling and singing. All his field-hands and coolies knew him for the kindest of masters.

The young couple had not been married a month, when a great prince, a member of the reigning house, visited the Lord of Echizen in his province. Report had it that this royal prince was in reality an emissary from the Emperor, for at this time the country was torn with the dissensions of Imperialist and Bakufu. It was well known that the Daimio of Echizen owed his office of shogunate premier to the Mikado himself, and that he was secretly in sympathy with the Imperialists. Consequently there were great banquets and entertainments given in the Province of Echizen when a prince of the royal family condescended to visit the Mikado's vassal, the Daimio of Echizen. The whole province wore a gala aspect, and the streets of the principal cities were constantly enlivened by the passing parades and cortèges of the retainers of the visiting prince.

Owing to the presence of his august guest, the Lord of Echizen was obliged to send a courier to Yedo with proper apologies for not presenting himself before the Shogun at this time. He showed his confidence in Kwacho by bestowing upon him the honor of this important mission.

The young farmer, while naturally loath to leave his young bride of a month, yet, mindful of the great honor, started at once for the Shogun's capital. Thus Ohano was left at home alone.

Being but fifteen years old, she was fond of gayety, of music and dancing, and it was her dearest wish to visit the capital city of the province, that she might see the gorgeous parade of the nobles. With her husband gone, however, she was forced to deny herself this pleasure, and had to remain at home in seclusion under the charge of an elderly but foolish maid. Ohano became lonely and restless. She wearied of sitting in the house, thinking of Kwacho; and it was tiresome, too, to wander about the farm fields and watch the coolies and laborers. Ohano pined for a little of that excitement so precious to her butterfly heart. Much thought of the capital gayeties, and much conversation with the foolish maid, finally wrought a result.

Ohano would put on her prettiest and gayest of gowns to visit the capital alone, just as though she were a maiden and not a matron who should have had the company of her husband.

As the city was not a great distance away, they could use a comfortable kurumma which would hold them both. Four of the field coolies could be spared as kurumma carriers. In delight the foolish maid dressed her mistress, by this time all rosy with pleasurable excitement and anticipation. The adventure pleased them both, though the foolish mistress assured the foolish maid repeatedly that they would go but to the edge of the city. Thus they could see the great parade of the royal prince pass out of the city gates, for this was the day on which the prince was to leave Echizen and return to Kyoto. All his splendid retinue would accompany him. It was only once in a lifetime one was afforded the opportunity of such a sight, Ohano declared.

They started from the farm gleefully. All the way mistress and maid chatted and laughed in enjoyment. Before they had reached the edge of the city a countryman told them the royal cortège was even then passing through the city gates, and that they must leave the road in haste, for the parade would reach their portion of the highway in a few minutes.

The foolish maid suggested that they alight from the kurumma, that they might have a still better view of the parade. So after the maid the rosy-cheeked little bride, with her eyes dancing and shining, her red lips apart, her childish face all gleaming with pleased curiosity, swung lightly to the ground also.

They were just in time, for the royal parade had taken the road, and the outriders were already in view, so that the kurumma carriers were forced to drag their vehicle aside and fall upon their faces in the dust. The foolish maid, following their example, hid her face on the ground so that she lost sight of that she had come far to see. Ohano, however, less agitated than her servants, instead of prostrating herself at the side of the road, retired to a little bluff near the roadside. She thought she was far enough from the highway to be unseen; but as she happened to be standing on a sloping elevation, and her gay dress made a bright spot of color against the landscape, she was perfectly visible to such of the cortège as chanced to look in her direction.

Very slowly and leisurely the train proceeded. Nobles, samurai, vassals, retainers, attendants, the personal train of each principal samurai, prancing horses, lacquered litters, norimonos, bearing the wives and concubines of the princely staff, banners and streamers and glittering breastplates, all these filed slowly by and dazzled the eyes of the little rustic Ohano.

Then suddenly she felt her knees become weak, hands trembled, while a great flame rushed to her giddy little head. She became conscious of the fact that the train had suddenly halted, and that the bamboo hangings of a gilded norimon had parted. As the curtains of the norimon were slowly lifted, the six stout-legged retainers carrying the vehicle came to a standstill, while one of them, apparently receiving an order, deftly drew the hangings from side to side, revealing the personage within. The norimon's occupant had raised himself lazily on his elbow and turned about sidewise in his carriage. His eyes were languorous and sleepy, slow and sensuous in their glance. They looked out now over the heads of the retainers, upward toward the small bluff upon which stood Ohano.

For some reason, perhaps because she saw something warmer than menace in the eyes of this indolent individual, Ohano smiled half unconsciously. Her little white teeth gleamed between her rosy lips. She appeared very bewitching as she stood there in her flowered gown in the sunlight.

A moment later something extraordinary happened to Ohano. She knew that stout arms had seized her, that her eyes were suddenly bound with linen, and then that she was lifted from her feet. Her giddy senses reeled to a dizzy unconsciousness.

When next she opened her eyes, she found that all was darkness about her. Consciousness came to her very slowly. She knew from the swaying movement of what seemed the soft couch upon which she lay that she was being carried somewhere. Ohano put out a fearful little hand, and it touched—a face! At that she sat up crying out in fright. Then the person who lay beside her stretched out hands toward her, and she was suddenly drawn down into his arms. He whispered in her ear, and his voice was like that of one speaking to her in a dream.

"Fear nothing, little dove. You are safe with me in my norimon. But to see you was to desire you. Do not tremble so. You will appreciate the honor I have done you, when you realize it. You shall be the favorite concubine of the Prince of Nijo, and never a wish of your heart or eyes shall be denied by me."

She could not stir, so close he held her.

"It is so dark," she cried breathlessly, "and I am afraid. O-O-most h-h-honorable prince."

"It is night, pretty dove; but if I part the curtains of my norimon, the august moon will lend us joyful light. Will you then cease to tremble and to fear me?"

She began to sob weakly, and through her childish brain just then filtered the vague thought of Kwacho. She was like one enmeshed in a dream nightmare. He who lay beside her laughed softly, and sought to wipe away her tears with his sensuous lips.

"Tears are for the sad and homely. Never for the Jewel of Nijo! Well, with his own august lips he wipes them away from the pretty dove's face. So and so!"

Yamada Kwacho returned to Echizen one week later. As became a bridegroom, the young husband had gone first to his home, intending to report to his prince immediately afterward. He entered the little farm-house with a joyous step and an eager, expectant face. He left the house like one shot from a cannon, on a mad run for the city. His brain whirled. He could not see. He could not think. He had a dim memory of having rushed upon the foolish maid like one demented, of listening with gaping mouth to the tale she told; then of thrusting her from him with such force that she fell to the floor in a heap.

Forgetting the respect due his lordship, the young farmer burst into the Daimio of Echizen's presence. He had none of the samurai calm, and his whole form fairly shook and swayed with the strength of his emotions.

The Lord of Echizen thrust forward a startled face.

"News from the shogunate, Yamada Kwacho?" he cried, fearing from the aspect of the youth that some treachery had been done his political party. In disjointed sentences, words coming through his teeth with effort because of his heavy breathing, the young farmer told his lord of the kidnapping of his bride, and recalled to him that promise of aid when necessity should demand it.

The young husband pleaded not in vain. Grieved, insulted, and incensed, the Daimio of Echizen journeyed in person to the Mikado's city of Kyoto, and straight to his August Majesty himself went the story of the farmer of Echizen. After this there was a great search made through the palaces and harems of the Prince of Nijo. Five months later Ohano was found and returned to her husband, Yamada Kwacho.

Three months had scarcely passed before the bells of the Imperial City rang out a joyous chime. The consort of the Prince of Nijo had given birth to a royal princess. On that same day, in the little farm-house of Yamada Kwacho, one more female citizen was added to the Province of Echizen, and Ohano became a mother.

I

THE CHILD OF THE SUN

On the shore of Hayama, in a little village two hours' ride by train from Tokyo, there stood a sumptuous villa, the summer residence of the Prince of Nijo, though Nijo himself was seldom seen there. Dissolute and dissipated by nature and cultivation, he preferred the gayeties and excitements of the Imperial Court. Here, however, had resided ever since the year of the Restoration his mother, the Empress Dowager, a noble and high-souled woman, who preferred the old-fashioned conservatism and beauty of her country palace to the modern and garish court.

The decorations of her palace, the style of her robes, and those of her attendants, were entirely of the old time. This was in pleasing contrast to the customs of the new Empress, who had adopted the foreign style. In the Imperial Court in its new Tokyo home, there was the heavy perfume of the choicest roses and violets, but in the palace of the old Empress Dowager there was the subtle, faint aroma of sweet umegaku and tambo.

Fuji, the queenly mountain, wrapped about in its glorious garment of snow, mellowed by the touch of the sun, could be seen from her seat. On all sides of the palace grounds there were valleys and sloping hills. Within the stone walls which encircled the palace like a fortress there were gardens of wondrous beauty.

The palace itself was of simple and old-fashioned architecture. It faced to the east, and its towers and turrets were of gold. Its shojis were large and so clear that the sunlight pierced through them, flooding the interior. The floors were covered with soft sweet tatamis—rush mats; the decorations on the screens and panels of the sliding doors were subdued and refined though works of art.

It was in this palace that the daughter of the Prince of Nijo spent her childhood. She was called Sado-ko, after her mother, who had died in giving her birth. Her father after his presence at a perfunctory feast given in honor of the birth of the princess had returned immediately to his pleasures in the capital, and Sado-ko was left in the charge of her grandmother, the Dowager Empress.

Great was the love existing between these two. All that was noblest in the character and nature of the young princess was fostered by the old Empress. The qualities for which she became noted in after years were the chilling work of those who, after the death of her grandmother, were given charge of Sado-ko.

In early childhood Sado-ko was wont to run with fleet feet about the castle gardens, chasing the gloriously hued butterflies. They flew about her in great numbers, for they were importations to the palace as tame as home birds. They knew the little princess would do them no harm, and so they fluttered lightly to her finger, her head, her shoulder, even to her red lips. Sado-ko loved them dearly, just as she adored the gardens and the goddess-like Fuji,—her first sight upon arising in the morning. She loved, too, the quiet, retired beauty of her life, with its freedom inside the dark stone walls. But more than these things she loved the Empress Dowager.

Until she was twelve years of age, she knew no other life than that encompassed by the walls of the palace grounds. Beyond them she had been told there was another life, turbulent, restless, troublous. The walls looked forbidding. How much worse must be the world outside them, and beyond the wide stretch of land and water that faded into misty outline!

Within were sunshine, birds, flowers, gentle words, and soft caressing smiles. Without, a cruel, cold world waiting to snuff out the warmth and sunshine of her nature. All this was taught to Sado-ko by the old Empress Dowager, who in her old age had become selfish. This was the way in which she sought to keep with her the heart and soul of the companion of her old age,—the child she loved. Even after she had passed away, she knew that the thoughts of the princess would remain with her though her soul should have flown. Thus she paved the way for a companionship in death as in life, as was the custom with her ancient ancestors.

The children of the Empress Dowager had disappointed her. The Emperor was occupied with the cares of the nation and the strenuous conditions of the times, Nijo was almost imbecile from dissipation, her only daughter had been married into the Tokugawa family, and was practically separated from her own kin. There was none left to share companionship with the old Empress, until the little Sado-ko had come. She was the sole princess of the Nijo family recognized by the Empress, for Western morality having sifted its way into the Japanese court, the children of Nijo by his concubines were regarded as illegitimate by the heads of the royal family, although they were treated with the honor due their blood and rank. Sado-ko was motherless. The Empress Dowager was her natural and legal guardian, and to her grandmother she was given.

For ten years, then, these two—the very old Empress and the very young princess—lived together. Because she was not at all of an inquisitive mind, and believed implicitly all that her grandmother told her, the child was perfectly contented with the simple companionship of the Empress, her butterflies, flowers, and birds. But her grandmother was too old to run with her about the gardens, and ofttimes the birds, and the butterflies too, flew over the stone wall and disappeared, to the tearful anxiety of the little princess, who was sure they would meet great harm.

As the children of the retainers of the Empress Dowager were not permitted to visit the private gardens of the palace, Sado-ko had grown up without playmates of her own age. She was being reared in that seclusion befitting a descendant of the sun-goddess, and in quite the ancient style to which her grandmother still clung. So it was only those attendants who waited upon the person of the Dowager Empress who saw the little princess herself. She could have counted upon her ten pink fingers the number of personages with whom she was acquainted. There were the four grim samurai guards of the palace gates, the three elderly maids of honor to the Empress, and her own personal maid and nurse Onatsu-no, in addition to the palace servants and the gardener.

But one eventful day in the month of June, a new personage suddenly introduced himself to Sado-ko. She had been listening drowsily for a long time on the wide balcony of the palace to her grandmother's reading aloud of ancient Chinese poems, when suddenly a swarm of her own butterflies flew by, all seemingly following the lead of a purple-hued stranger. Instantly Sado-ko left her guardian's side in pursuit, her net swinging in her hand. She had seldom experienced any trouble in catching her own butterflies, but the stranger flew in an entirely new direction. Through a field of iris and across an orchard Sado-ko followed the flight of the butterflies, until she came to a wall, over which the purple visitor flew.

Flushed and disappointed the princess sat down breathlessly on the grass beneath a cherry tree. She had been seated but a moment, when the tree above her began to shake and a score of ripe cherries descended upon her head. She sprang to her feet, and looking upward saw a roguish face peering down at her from the cherry tree. The face belonged to a boy of possibly fourteen years. He was laughing with delight at the amazed and frightened face of the little princess, and he kept pelting her with cherries, some of which actually broke on her small Imperial person. As, however, Sado-ko continued to gaze up at him in that frightened manner, he sprang to the ground, rolled himself about on the grass for a spell, and then turned several somersaults so grotesque that Sado-ko forgot her fear and burst into childish laughter, clapping her hands delightedly as he came to his feet before her. They were both laughing heartily now, as they surveyed each other. The boy's sleeves and the front of his obi were filled with cherries, so that his figure was a succession of grotesque bunches. There were cherry stains, too, on his face, particularly in the region of his laughing mouth, through which Sado-ko saw the whitest of teeth gleaming. He had brown eyes, and soft silky hair, unshaven in the centre of his head, as was the case with the palace attendants. Gradually as the princess surveyed him she became grave.

"Who are you?" she said at last. "What is your honorable name, and where do you live?"

"I am Kamura Junzo," said the boy, "and I live over yonder." He waved his hand toward the wall.

"On the other side?" inquired Sado-ko in an awed voice. He nodded.

"I know who you are," he continued.

"I am the Princess Sado-ko," said the child, gravely.

"Yes," said the boy, "and the august Sun was your ancestor. You live shut up in this place all alone, and no one plays with you."

"I have my honorable dear birds and butterflies," she said.

He looked at her curiously.

"Yes, I have heard you singing to them."

"And you wished also to see me?" she questioned.

"Yes." He flushed boyishly, and then added with Spartan honesty, "Also I wanted some of your cherries."

"They are very good," said the princess.

"Oh, yes, there are none so good without."

"Did the guards deign to let you pass through the gates?"

"No." A pause, then: "I deigned to climb over the wall."

"Some day," said Sado-ko, wistfully, "her Majesty says a prince will fly over the walls and carry me away. Perhaps you are that prince."

"Oh, no; I am not a prince, but if you wish, I will play that I am one."

"How is that?" she asked, bewildered.

"This cherry tree will be your august castle. I will come over the wall, and you must run around the castle to escape me. I will pursue you, and then I will carry you off from this dark and lonesome prison over the walls to the beautiful world outside."

"But it is not a lonesome prison here," said the princess, "and outside it is very cold and miserable, for her Majesty has told me so."

"Oh, well, let us play it is so."

And so they played together until past noon, when the maid and gardener were both sent to seek the Princess Sado-ko, who was chasing butterflies. They rescued her just as the "prince" was about to carry her over the walls, upon the top of which he had placed her, by climbing up in the cherry tree and across a bough which sloped to the wall.

The rescued princess stamped her foot angrily at the gardener when he threatened the boy, who laughed jeeringly from the top of the wall; and she scolded the maid when that menial drew her by the hand from the scene. She would not leave the vicinity of the wall until the boy had disappeared completely, which he did by jumping off to the other side. Then she burst into tears for fear he had come to harm in the wicked world without.

Thereafter a close watch was kept upon her movements, and she was not permitted to go near that portion of the walls where stood the cherry-tree castle. Often she heard the boy whistling from that direction, and once she awoke in the night, because she had dreamed that he was calling her name, "Sado-ko! Sado-ko!" After that life was a little more lonesome for the Child of the Sun.

II

An Emperor's Promise

On a cold morning in the month of January the Empress Dowager died. She had returned from a ceremony of the thirtieth anniversary of the death of her late consort. Exhausted, broken, and ill, she had come back to her country-seat, her visit to Kyoto having been too much for her strength.

That night messengers went in haste to the capital, and the following morning brought to the bedside of the dying Empress her son, the Emperor, and his consort.

All night long the little Princess Sado-ko crouched in the darkness of her room alone. Wide-eyed and tearless, she looked out from her shoji at the ghostly snow which shrouded her beloved trees and flowers in so cold and chilly a garment, eerily touched by the moon-rays. She heard, without heeding, the movement and stir within the palace; the muffled beat of a drum without quickly hushed. Early in the gray morning the royal visitors arrived. Sado-ko knew that some catastrophe was about to fall upon the palace and her beloved grandmother, and so she waited through the night for the end.

She did not know that below in the sick chamber the heartbroken Emperor knelt on his knees by the side of his mother and besought her, like any ordinary man, to speak but one word to him, to express but one wish ere she must leave him. The Dowager Empress opened her tired eyes, attempting to speak. She could only murmur in the faintest of voices, so that her son scarcely caught the words:—

"Sado-ko—Pray thee to care for—Sado-ko!"

Then her eyes closed as though the effort at speech had been too much for her, but the Emperor knew that she heard the words he spoke into her ears.

"Divine mother, the Princess Sado-ko shall have my personal care. She shall be nurtured and cared for as the highest princess in Japan, and when she has attained to a fitting age the greatest honor in my power shall be given to her."

There was no further sign from the Dowager Empress.

"Princess!" called a voice penetrating the darkened room, by the shoji of which the child crouched dully. "Noble princess!"

Sado-ko did not stir, though she looked with wide eyes toward the sliding door through which came her maiden Natsu, holding carefully above her head a lighted andon. She had not seen the little figure by the shoji, and she shuffled toward the couch. A startled exclamation escaped her when she discovered that the couch was empty. At that the princess called to her in a strange voice, which seemed somehow unlike her own.

"I am here, honorable maid."

The woman hastened forward, the light still swinging over her head. She stopped aghast before the still little figure of the princess, who was, she could see, fully dressed. It was plain that the child had robed herself with her own hands, after she had left her for the night.

The maid set the andon down, then touched the floor with her head. After her obeisance she went nearer to Sado-ko, and spoke with the familiarity which years in the child's service had allowed her.

"Thou art not unrobed, noble princess!"

"I have not slept," said the child, quietly.

The maid seized her hands with an exclamation of pity.

"The hands are like ice!" she exclaimed immediately. "Exalted princess, you are ill!"

"No," said Sado-ko, shaking her head, "I am not ill, Natsu-no. But tell me your mission. Why do you come so early to my chamber?"

There was nothing childlike now in the grave glance of Sado-ko's eyes. She seemed to have aged over night. At her words the maid burst into tears, beat her hands against her breast, and finally bent her head to the floor. The princess waited in silence until the maid had regained somewhat of her composure. Then she said severely, quite in the manner of her august grandparent:—

"Maiden, such emotion is unseemly. Speak your mission, if you please."

"Oh, august princess, her Imperial Majesty—" She fell to weeping again.

Sado-ko leaned forward, and placing her hand on the maid's shoulder, peered into her face.

"—is dead?" she said in a whisper.

The maid's head bowed forward mutely. After that there was a long silence. Then Sado-ko arose to her feet, her hands pressed to her face on either side. Her eyes, between her little parted fingers, were staring out in shocked horror. Her strange silence stilled the sobbing maid, who tremulously arose.

"And if it please thee, noble princess," she said, "his August Majesty is below and commands thy immediate presence."

Sado-ko did not speak or move. The maid falteringly touched one of the drooping sleeves.

"Nay, do not look so, sweet mistress," she implored; "the gods will not desert you. His Majesty himself has deigned to adopt thee, and to-morrow thou wilt go to the great capital as his ward."

Sado-ko's hands fell from her face. Her voice was not childlike, and quite hoarse.

"Pray thee, lead me below, honorable maid."

IT WAS LIGHTER NOW IN the palace, for a wan sun was creeping upward in the pale heavens. There were signs of a dreary day about to dawn. Through the winding corridors of the palace the princess and the maid moved toward the august chamber of death. At its door they paused and the princess's hand dropped from that of the maid. Having permitted her attendant to push the sliding doors apart, she entered the chamber alone. Without, the maid bent her face to the mats, stifling her sobs in her sleeves. Within, the little princess hesitated a moment in doubt, then rushed to the death couch, threw herself down by the still form there, and unmindful of those within, encircled it with her arms. But no cry escaped her lips, for well had she been bred as a Daughter of the Sun-god by the old Empress Dowager.

The days that followed were hazy and unreal to Sado-ko. Strange women and men, with cold impassive faces, were about her at all times. She could scarcely tell one from the other, and it wearied her to be forced to listen to their words of caution and counsel. Then she made a journey. Strangely enough, when she was lifted into the covered palanquin and the curtains drawn about her, she knew that now she was to be carried beyond the gray palace walls. The journey was made at night, and the tired little princess slept throughout it, so that she was spared the tediousness of time.

In the morning her eyes opened upon a new world. As the day streamed through the bamboo curtains of her norimon, she pushed them aside, to see that they were passing along what seemed to be a stone road, upon either side of which were endless buildings unlike anything she had ever seen before. Although there were throngs of people everywhere, a strange and solemn silence prevailed, as the norimon and parade of the princess passed along, and the people bent their heads to the earth. Sado-ko could see that many of the women and some of the men wept. She did not know that the whole nation had gone into mourning for the one she had loved so well.

Sado-ko, passive and unquestioning, saw the great funeral of the Empress Dowager; a dumb little shadow, she lingered with other relatives in the hall for the mourners, and still, with little understanding, she was carried in her norimon under the escort given only to a royal princess, through a bamboo grove and over the Yumento Ukibashi— "The Bridge of Dreams." The mortuary hall was reached. The Empress Dowager, whose dearest wish had been to be buried close to her summer palace, where she had spent her declining years, was interred far away from it among the tombs of her thousand ancestors.

III

Masago

From a poor but honored farmer of Echizen, Yamada Kwacho had grown to be a rich and prominent merchant of Tokyo. At the advice of the Lord of Echizen, Kwacho had gone to Tokyo soon after the Restoration, where, taking advantage of the modern craze for Western things then raging in the capital, he had invested the price of his little farm in one of the first "European" stores in Tokyo. His business had prospered and grown rapidly to huge dimensions. Now, while Kwacho was still in the prime of life, he found himself richer in worldly wealth than his former master the Lord of Echizen even in his best days.

The young farmer of Echizen had been content to remain in his humble class, though honors were offered him by his lord. The rich and prominent merchant of Tokyo was still at heart the conservative and independent young farmer of Echizen. Despite the fact that his great wealth would have purchased for him an entrée to a high society, Kwacho made no effort to emerge from his life of quiet and obscure ease. Possibly, too, an experience of his early married life caused him to look askance and with disfavor upon the lives of the society people. At all events a pretty home in a suburb of Tokyo, and the society of a few simple neighbors, quite contented him.

Whether the ambitions of Ohano kept the level of those of her husband, was not a matter of any determination. The mistress of a comfortable home, the comely wife of a respected citizen, and the mother of five sons and one daughter, she appeared contented with her lot.

There had always been a weak and soft element in the character of Ohano, however. In youth it had come near to being the cause of her complete ruin. But for the sturdy nature of her husband, Ohano might never have recovered morally. In latter years this weakness of disposition took the form of an almost childish delight in dwelling secretly in her own mind upon experiences in her life which she would not have breathed aloud even to her favorite god, much less to her sombre husband. Strangely enough, too, Ohano had far more affection for her daughter than for her sons,—a most uncommon thing in a Japanese woman.

As a little girl, Masago had been remarkable chiefly for her docile and quiet ways. This apathy of nature, peculiar in a child of her class, had been variously regarded by the teachers in the public school she had attended. Some had pronounced her dull and even sullen, while others insisted that her impassiveness showed an innate refinement and delicacy of birth and caste. Masago was very pretty after a delicate Yamato fashion. Unlike her sturdy young brothers, round-faced, rugged, and brimming over with health and spirits, Masago was oval-faced, her eyes were long and dreamy, her mouth small, the lips thin and prettily curved. Her skin was of a fine texture, and her little hands were quite as beautiful as those of the princesses who attended the Peeresses' school.

Masago's schoolmates thought her quiet disposition indicative of secretiveness and even slyness. She had never been known to express herself on any question, though no one gave closer attention to any matter under controversy than she. The consequence was that as she grew older her girl friends, at first sceptical and dubious of her quiet, unexpressive face, finally ended in confiding to her their various secrets; for well they knew that while they might expect no exchange of confidences, their secrets were well guarded within Masago's silent little head and as safe as if unspoken.

Ohano, too, was quick to take advantage of the child's listening talent and receptive mind. In spite of the fact that Masago was coming to an age when all such confidences should have been strictly kept from her, Ohano found herself gradually pouring out to her daughter those fascinating and forbidden secrets which still remained in her mind. She would sit opposite her daughter for hours at a time and describe graphically the palaces of Kyoto. It would have occurred to one older than Masago that, for one in her caste, Ohano's knowledge of these places was unusual. But the child asked few questions and appeared to be absorbed in her mother's glowing narrative. Only once she said, lifting her strange long eyes to her mother's face:—

"It is in the palace I belong, mother, is it not?" And before Ohano was conscious of her words she had replied:—

"There, indeed, you belong of right, Masago."

When Masago had reached her seventeenth year, she expressed her first independent wish to her family. It was that she be sent to a finishing school in Kyoto.

At her suggestion, made directly to him, Kwacho was disgruntled. She had had sufficient education for a maiden of her class, he insisted. What was more, he desired her to make an early marriage and had already begun negotiations for her betrothal.

Masago listened to her father's words without replying, beyond a wordless bow of submission to his will. She did not argue the matter with him, since she knew that Ohano, without diplomacy and craft, had yet great influence with Kwacho. So the young girl went quietly to her mother, whom she found happily employed in washing a small barking chin on the rear veranda of the house. She looked back smilingly at her daughter over her shoulder as she rubbed the dog's twitching little body.

"He is white enough," said Masago, quietly, indicating the chin with a slight movement of her head. At this verdict Ohano released the dog. He darted about the veranda for a moment, shaking his still wet little body, then rushed through the shoji indoors, disappearing under a mat over a warm hibachi, where he shivered in comfort.

Ohano emptied out the water across a flower bed, and unrolled her sleeves. She was flushed with her exercise, and the water had splashed her gown. Her hair, too, was dishevelled, but she was the picture of the healthy housewife, as she turned to her daughter.

The latter, in her perfect neatness, made a contrast to the mother, who surveyed her with fond approval.

"Well, Masago, have you finished your embroidery?" she asked pleasantly.

The girl shook her head silently.

"Go, then; get your frame now," said Ohano, "and we will work together."

"No," said Masago, seating herself on a veranda mat, and leaning back against the railing, "I don't want to work. I want to talk to you."

Ohano's plump body quickly seated itself opposite Masago. The opportunity for a morning gossip with Masago was something she never denied herself.

She had just opened her mouth to begin, When Masago quietly put her hand over the red orifice.

"No; do not speak for a moment, mother, but listen to me."

Masago smiled faintly at the expression in her mother's eyes and continued rapidly:—

"Listen. I am seventeen years now,—old enough, almost, my father says, to be married. But I do not wish to marry."

"But—" began Ohano.

"No; do not interrupt me. I want to go away to school,—a private school in Kyoto, where other rich men send their daughters, and where I, too, can sometimes see those palaces and maybe the noble ladies and gentlemen you have told me so much about."

"But, Masago, every maiden of your age wishes to marry; and your father has chosen—"

"Let me finish, if you please, or I will not talk to you at all. I do not know why it is, but I have no desire to marry; and sometimes I feel like one who is stifling in this miserable little town. Why should we, who have more wealth than many of those in Tokyo who live in palaces, be caged up here, like birds with clipped wings? What is the use of having that wealth if we may not use it? Oh, there are so many joyful happenings in the capital every day and every night. I read about it in those papers which father brings home sometimes from Tokyo. The city is so gay and brilliant, mother, and there are so many peculiar foreigners to see. I was made for such a place—not for this dull, quiet town. Why, I would even be content to see all this as an outsider, but to have to remain here when—Oh!"

She struck her hands together with an eloquent motion. Ohano stared at her aghast, regarding her flushing face and snapping eyes.

"Oh, mother," she continued, "many people say I do not belong here. They recognize my difference from themselves,—everybody here. You know it is so. Ever since I was a little girl when you would tell me the fairy tales of those palaces in Kyoto—"

"They were not fairy tales," said Ohano, gently.

"No, but I thought them so—then. And I imagined that some day the gods would befriend me, and that I would belong to that joyful world of which you spoke. And now to come to seventeen years and to be given right away in marriage to some foolish youth before I have had any chance to see—"

Her voice broke, and her emotion was so unusual a thing that Ohano could not bear to see it. Both her heart and tongue were stirred.

"You have a right to see it," she said. "You belong to it—are a part of it, Masago. Your own father is—"

She clapped her hands over her mouth in consternation and sudden fright at what she was about to divulge.

Masago became very white, her eyes dilated, her thin nostrils quivered. She fixed her strange, long eyes full on those of her mother. Then she seized her by the shoulders. She spoke in a whisper:—

"You have something to tell me. Now—speak at once."

Half an hour later Masago was alone on the veranda of her home. She sat in an attitude of intense absorption. Her downcast eyes were looking at the slender fingers of her hands, spread out in her lap. They were thin, shapely little fingers, the nails rosy and perfect in shape. Masago had been studying them absently for some time. Suddenly she held up one little hand, then slowly brought it to her face.

"That was the reason they were so beautiful—my hands!" she said softly.

That night Ohano would not let her husband sleep until he had made her a promise. They lay on their respective mattresses under the same mosquito netting. It was quite in vain for Kwacho to sleep while the voice of Ohano droned on. After listening for fully two hours to a steady stream of childish eloquence and reproach, and answering only in gruff monosyllables, he sprang up in bed and demanded of his better half whether she intended to remain awake all night. Whereat that small but stubborn individual raised herself also, and, propping her elbows on her knees, informed the irate Kwacho that such was her intention, and that, in fact, she did not expect to sleep any night again until he had made some concession to the ambition of their only daughter, which, after all, was a most praiseworthy one,—a desire for more learning.

Kwacho's answer was not the result of a sudden appreciation of Masago's virtues, but he was sleepy and tired, too. There was much to be done at the store on the morrow, and Ohano's suggestion that she intended to keep awake for other nights was not a relishing prospect.

"She shall go on one condition," he said.

"Yes?" eagerly inquired his wife.

"That she is first betrothed to Kamura Junzo."

"There will be no trouble as to that," said Ohano, with conviction, and lying down drew the quilt over her. A few minutes later the twain were at rest.

IV

A Betrothal

The following morning an early messenger brought a letter to the Kamura residence. The family were at breakfast, but as the messenger came from the elder Kamura's old Echizen friend, Yamada Kwacho, it was opened and read at once. Its contents, while surprising, were most pleasing to the family. Kwacho made an overture to contract a betrothal between their eldest son, Junzo, and his only daughter, Masago.

Junzo at this time was in Tokyo, where he had been living ever since he had returned from abroad. He was winning fame for himself as a sculptor,—an art quite new to Japan in its Western form,—and the family were proud of his achievements. This new mark of compliment from their esteemed friend, the wealthy Mr. Yamada, naturally flattered the Kamura family immensely. The messenger was sent back to the Yamada house with as gracious letter as the one received, and gifts of flowers and tea. The invitation of Mr. Yamada for a conference at his house the day following, in which the young couple might also have an opportunity of seeing each other and becoming acquainted, was accepted. Another messenger was despatched at once to Junzo in Tokyo, and the family congratulated themselves upon what they considered their good fortune.

Junzo read his father's letter with a degree of irritation altogether out of keeping with the pride in the proposal manifested by the rest of his family. An extraordinary piece of fortune had recently come to Junzo, and the subject of his marriage seemed a matter of trivial importance beside it. He had, in fact, been commissioned to make a statue of the Prince Komatzu, the war hero of the time, who had distinguished himself by his brave conduct in the Formosa affair. Junzo knew that upon this work his future career would depend, and that should he please his illustrious patron he would doubtless have an opportunity of doing more work for the court; for at this time the nobility of Japan emulated everything modern and Western, and it had become the fashion for the gentlemen of the court to sit for their portraits in oil, though as yet none of the ladies had gone quite so far.

Junzo's impatience, therefore, at his father's summons to return home for the consummation of his betrothal to a young lady whom he had never seen, may be surmised. Being a well-bred and obedient son, however, he departed at once for his home, breaking a number of engagements in so doing.

As the train from Tokyo carried Junzo to Kamakura, the young man, while watching the flying landscape from his window, thought with some natural curiosity of his bride to be. Her father and mother he had met. Upon two or three occasions he had seen her little brothers playing in the fields. His active imagination soon pictured Masago. She would, of course, be plump and rosy-cheeked like her mother, pretty perhaps, thought Junzo, but lacking in that grace and spirituality that to him was the ideal of true beauty.

When his own grandsires had been samurai in the service of the Lords of Echizen, this girl's ancestors had tilled the soil. Still, times were changed. The samurai had fallen, and the tradesman and farmer had risen. Now the descendants of the samurai drew the jinrikisha containing the fat merchant, or policed the streets of big cities for the glory of still wearing a sword. Moreover, the elder Kamura was in sympathy with the modern spirit of the times, and had accepted favors from the hand of Yamada Kwacho. Besides, the latter had not been without honor in Echizen; and, after all, his own family—the once proud samurai family of Kamura—were now but simple citizens, nothing more.

"The Restoration was right and just," said Junzo, and smoothed out the frown from his patrician face. "And after all," he added to his thought, "this girl of the people will be a more fitting wife than a woman of modern fancies, such as have become the ladies of caste."

Masago's aspect pleased, surprised—nay, quite bewildered Junzo. When at the look-at meeting she had raised her head finally from its low obeisance, Junzo had been startled at its delicate beauty. It shocked him to see a flower so exquisitely lovely and delicate surrounded by relatives so completely plebeian.

During the entire visit Junzo found his eyes constantly straying toward his betrothed. When she moved about the room, and with her own hands served him tea, he noted with delight her grace of movement, and the symmetry of her figure.

When tea had been served and drunk, he found her close beside him. She had moved dutifully there at a signal from her father; and now, as his betrothed, she quietly filled the long-stemmed pipe for him, and lighted it at the hibachi. As he took it from her hands, their eyes met for the first time. Junzo, though thrilled by the glance of her eyes, felt curiously enough repulsed. There was something forbidding, almost menacing, in their glance. A moment later the long lashes were shielding them. Then the young man noted that she had not as much as changed color, but still was calmly white and unmoved. A feeling of uneasiness possessed him. His delight in her beauty was chilled.

Once only throughout the afternoon did she show interest in the conversation. This was when Junzo had told his father-in-law to be, of a prospective visit to court to make a statue of a national hero. Then she had raised her head suddenly, and Junzo had stumbled over his words in the glow of artistic appreciation he felt of the beautiful pink color flooding her face.

The elder Kamura thought his son's modesty in not mentioning the fact of the commission he had already received unnecessary in a family soon to become his own; and so he said, as he tapped the ashes from his pipe on the hibachi:—

"My son has been commanded to make a statue of his Imperial Highness the Prince Komatzu."

The little cup which Masago had lifted toward her lips fell suddenly from her hand, its contents spilling on the tray. She seemed scarcely conscious of its fall, as she turned an eager and flushed face toward Kamura. She spoke for the first time, repeating half mechanically his words:—

"The Prince Komatzu—"

"Yes," said Kamura, affably, "a cousin of his Imperial Majesty," and he bowed his head to the mats in old-fashioned deference to the name of the Mikado.

"Why," spoke up the simple Ohano, her eyes wide and bright, "we have his august picture."

Her husband looked at her in astonishment.

"You have a picture of his Highness?" he inquired incredulously. "How is that possible, Ohano?"

"Masago cut it from a Chinese magazine you brought home last month," said the wife, "and it was such a beautiful picture she has put it away among her treasures, have you not, Masago?"

The girl's eyes were downcast, and she did not raise them. She knew by the silence in the room that her answer was awaited by the company, but she could not move her lips to speak. Then she heard Junzo answering quietly for her:—

"He is certainly the most admirable hero we have, and one that it honors our nation to idolize."

His words were rewarded by a glance from the eyes she raised in timid gratitude. It was but for a moment; then her head was bent again.

For a week Junzo saw his fiancée daily. At the end of that time he accompanied her with her family a portion of the way to Kyoto, whither she went to attend school for a year. Junzo then proceeded alone to Tokyo, and on his journey back his musings of his future bride were as vague and unsatisfactory as when he had come.

V

Gossip of the Court

It was early afternoon. The ladies in the Komatzu palace were taking their noon-day siesta, and idly discussing the work of the artist, Kamura Junzo. Since he had become a favorite among them, many of the ladies wished that he could be retained in the palace a little longer.

As they sipped their amber tea indolently in one of the chambers of the palace, they gossiped with the freedom common to the women of the West rather than the East.

"Now," said the little Countess Matsuka, handing her cup to a page, "if we were only so fortunate as to have two Imperial heroes instead of one!"

A languorous beauty, swinging lazily in a Dutch hammock, raised herself upon an elbow.

"But the heroes nowadays are all heimins" (commoners), she said with soft scorn.

"Oh, Duchess Aoi," laughed a pretty young woman, who, more industrious, was working at an embroidery frame, "how can you say so? There are no heimins to-day."

"Oh, true," responded the other, crossly, "there is no caste to-day. The heimin has become the politician."

"Yes," said the pretty one at the frame, "and the politician rules and owns Nippon."

The Duchess Aoi sat up aggressively.

"You appear to have the confidence of the diplomats, O Lady Fuji-no," said she.

Fuji tossed her head in malicious silence.

"Noble ladies!" came the warning voice of the elderly mentor-chaperon. "It is too warm to engage the august voice in argument. Let us have music."

The Duchess Aoi shrugged her shapely shoulders.

"The court geishas are busy in the male quarters," she said, "and the foreign band has broken our ear-drums."

One of the ladies laughed.

"Besides," she added to Aoi's speech, "we don't want the foreign music in our private halls. It is enough for state occasions."

"I enjoy it augustly well," said a stiff little lady sitting uncomfortably in her Paris gown on an English chair, who bore the euphonious name of Yu-giri (Evening Mist). She was the only one of the company who wore European costume. The others were glad enough to revel in the comfortable enjoyment of the kimono.

"If her Royal Highness were not so augustly eccentric, *she* might set the example," said the Countess Matsuka, thoughtfully.

"Which Highness, countess?"

"There is only one Royal Highness in the palace now," said Lady Fuji, smiling up from her frame,—"the Princess Sado-ko."

Aoi tossed her head angrily. Her mother had been a concubine of one of the Imperial princes, and she was of the blood. Yet she was maid of honor to the Princess Sado-ko, for whom she had no love.

"And what example might *she* set?" Aoi inquired with evident disdain.

"That of sitting for her portrait to be painted," explained the Countess Matsuka.

All of the ladies now showed extreme interest in the subject, and several began to speak at once.

"Oh, but she would never countenance it!"

"She fairly despises the ways of us moderns."

"Just to think, it is in her power to keep our charming artist at court indefinitely."

"But how lovely to have all our pictures painted. We, of course, would all follow suit."

"—if she would only set the fashion."

"Well, ladies," said the Lady Fuji, "the princess is not our fashion-plate, surely. We do not follow her, it would seem. If we did—"

"We should live like cloistered priestesses," said the one in the hammock.

"Yes, seclude ourselves from the sight of the whole court," said she of the Paris gown.

"Then why need we await her august example?" asked the Lady Fuji.

"Because we are cowards—all," said the Countess Matsuka. "To sit for our pictures just like any of the barbarians is too much of an innovation for any of the humble ones to start at court."

"Well, then," said Fuji, "who is brave enough to suggest it to the princess? She is both conservative and unconventional, and who knows she might take a fancy to the idea and consent?"

"Well, suppose you suggest it to her."

"I? Oh, indeed, I am too honorably insignificant."

"Then you, countess."

"Oh no, indeed; I am still smarting under the sting of her little royal tongue."

"Ah, you are too fulsome in your flattery to her, countess," said Lady Fuji-no. "Diplomacy and tact with her Highness should take the form of frankness, even brusqueness."

"Yes," said the one in the hammock, sarcastically, "I noted the effect of your diplomacy the other morning."

Lady Fuji-no colored, and bent her head above her work.

"Oh, these days, these days!" groaned the elderly lady, who was both chaperon and mentor to the others. "Now, in my insignificant youth it would have been a crime of treason to speak with disrespect of a royal princess."

"But you see," was the quick retort, "what happened to your august days, Madame Bara. They are quite, quite snuffed out. To-day is—to-day! We are modern—Western—if it please you!"

"Yes," assented the Paris gown, "that is it exactly."

"While the Princess Sado-ko remains—Eastern."

Lady Fuji, at the frame, had found her voice again. The Duchess Aoi in the hammock closed her eyes contemptuously.

"The day is long," she said, "and our conversation most dull."

"Well, we have not solved the question yet," said the anxious little Countess Matsuka.

"Oh, let the artist go," yawned one of the company, who had not yet spoken.

There was a hubbub of dissent to this.

"And leave us to the mercies of Komatzu's dandies?"

"The artist fellow is entertaining. He is preferable to a geisha."

"Oh, what a comparison!"

"Well, ladies," said Madame Bara, soothingly, "you will soon be back in Tokyo."

"Yes, thank Shaka!"

"Summer creeps."

"The Prince Komatzu would not be flattered, ladies, at your boredom in his summer home," said Madame Bara.

"Then the prince should choose more entertaining gentlemen for his household," retorted Lady Fuji-no. "Now, in the palace Nijo—"

"Oh, it is well, well, to be in favor at the palace Nijo," said the

Duchess Aoi, meaningly; and instantly the several eyes of the company were focussed on the flushing face of Fuji, for it was quite well known that Nijo had shown her marked favor of late.

"For my part," said the chaperon didactically, "I should be honored to be the exalted guest of his Imperial Highness. Why surely, ladies, you will confess that without a doubt he is the most brilliant and noble gentleman of the court."

The Duchess Aoi turned her face away. A feverish color flushed her cheeks. She could not speak.

"He is just exactly like the statue that the artist has made of him," said Lady Fuji-no.

"But the statue is sublime," said Madame Bara.

"Yes. But it is marble, madame."

There was silence a moment, while the Lady Fuji carefully folded her work, then the Duchess Aoi turned her flushing face:—

"Is it any wonder that he is marble?" she said. "He is betrothed to the Princess Sado-ko."

"Poor prince!" said Lady Fuji.

VI

The Princess Sado-ko

While the ladies of the household of the Princess Sado-ko, and guests of her cousin the Prince Komatsu, were gossiping over their noonday tea, Kamura Junzo, alone, was wandering aimlessly about the palace gardens. He was melancholy and restless. Instead of being satisfied with his success, Junzo was disappointed. He could not have explained why this was so. His patron had been pleased with his work, he had received marked attention and favor from those in power at court, and finally was actually being petted by the ladies. Perhaps it was this latter enervating thing that rendered the young man disappointed and disgusted.

Court life had not proved, after all, what he had fancied and pictured. Nobility, such as he had anticipated, was there only in name. Here in this small court of the noblest prince of the blood, gossip and scandal buzzed like the swarming of bees.

Junzo did not wonder that the Princess Sado-ko kept herself in seclusion in her private wing of the palace. In spite of the curious tales he had heard of her eccentricities, he felt a glow of sympathy for her. Plainly she disapproved of the life about her.

As he strolled about the castle gardens, Junzo's memory carried him back into the days of his childhood. A picture grew up in his mind of a great stone wall and a cherry tree which drooped above it, and underneath the cherry tree a small, bewitching creature in a miniature kimono and the royal kanzashi in her hair.

He was smiling to himself in a tender, unconscious way, when he came to a bamboo gate, which served as entrance through the hedge of boxwood which divided the portion of the gardens in which he was from those Junzo knew were always reserved for the royal ladies of the family. Now he knew also that Komatsu was an orphan without sisters, and that his cousin Sado-ko was the only lady who ever occupied this portion of the palace.

Pausing before the gate, Junzo thought that as a boy he would not have hesitated to push it open and penetrate into the forbidden territory beyond. He would like now to take a peep into this garden of Sado-ko.

If he should chance to meet her, might he not crave mercy in the name of that game they had played as children together in the gardens of the palace Aoyama? She might be gracious still. So far it had not been his fortune to see her in the palace Komatzu, for she was seldom in the public places of the palace. He had an insatiable curiosity to see how she had changed since childhood.

So he stepped across into the private gardens, making his way toward the bamboo grove, through which he passed on toward the little river which he could see in a valley beyond, twisting and babbling like a brook. But when he came to the other end of the grove he perceived that the garden was unlike those of the palace Aoyama, which was softly enclosed on all sides with trees and bushes. Here the walks were sanded and the landscape scenery was in miniature. There were flower beds and clumps of bamboo. Stately white jars containing rare ferns were placed at intervals in the centre of the rounded lawns, while the walks were lined with pretty sea-shells and white pebbles.

Junzo soon realized that this was not a garden in which he could remain for long unobserved. He was about to retrace his steps when he perceived coming toward him along the path a young girl, whose arms were so full of blossoms that her face was partially hidden. As it was too late for him now to retreat, he stood where he was, respectfully waiting for her to approach.

She hastened up the path toward him, and as she appeared to be absorbed in her own meditations and had not so far glanced in his direction, Junzo stepped backward toward the grove, hoping she would pass by without seeing him. This she doubtless would have done had not the young man, as she came opposite, made an odd exclamation, and then stepped before her path. What he said was:—

"Masago!"

She raised a startled face to his and stood perfectly still before him in the path, the blossoms slowly dropping from her arms. That strange expression of mingled fear and amazement awoke chaotic memories in the mind of Junzo. It was Masago who stood before him, he felt sure; but some one other than Masago had once looked up into his face in the same startled fashion. It must have been a dream or fancy. He repeated her name:—

"Masago!" And then, "What do you here?"

"Who are you?" she asked in a low voice, her eyes travelling over his face. "What is your honorable name, and where do you come from?"

The very words had a ring of familiarity to the ears of Junzo. He felt like one in a dream, and answered almost mechanically:—

"I am Kamura Junzo. I come from—" He made a slight motion toward the adjoining gardens.

A slow pink glow grew up into her face and spread even to her little ears and whitest neck. Her eyes were shining, almost as if there were tears within them.

"Ah," she said softly, "I do remember you."

"We are betrothed," he said, passing his hand bewilderedly across his eyes.

"Betrothed?" she repeated in that sweet, low-toned voice.

"Yes, Masago. Do you not remember then?"

"But my name is not Masago," she said simply.

"Not Masago!" he repeated.

"No. I am the Princess Sado-ko."

After that there was a long silence between them. They looked into each other's faces without speaking. Then the young man found his voice.

"I thought the august sun had touched my brain," he said. "I knew that your face was familiar to me, and because you are the image of one to whom—"

He broke off, flushing under the glance of her soft, searching eyes.

"To whom you are betrothed," she finished quietly.

"Yes," he said.

"And her name is Masago?" she asked musingly.

"Yes."

"And she looks like me?" She raised her face, and looked at him somewhat wistfully.

"Sweet princess," he said, carried away by the expression within her eyes, "her beauty is like unto the moon's—cold, far, and distant, but yours—yours warms me like the glow of the sun. You are indeed the child of the sun-god."

She smiled faintly.

"Are you the artist-man of whom they speak?" she asked.

He bowed slightly, and she continued:—

"I have admired the very beautiful statue you have made of Prince Komatzu."

"I trust that it will please the people," he said simply.

"Nay, he has presented it as a gift to me," she said.

Junzo recalled the report of her betrothal to the Prince Komatzu, and he turned a trifle pale. Possibly she divined his thoughts, for she said:

"We are cousins."

"And will be—" He did not finish the sentence.

She changed the subject abruptly.

"You will be at the palace long?"

"Two more days."

"And then?"

"I will return home."

"Home?" She repeated the word in such a wistful, lingering tone. "You will go back to Kamakura?" she asked.

"Yes."

"My dear old home!" she said. And then, "You do not know what memories your presence recalls to me."

He could not take his eyes from her expressive face.

"I have not seen it since I was a child," she said. "Why do you go so soon?"

"My honorable commission ends."

"There may be others."

"I have no other," he replied simply.

"The ladies of the court would honorably like their pictures painted?" she essayed almost timidly.

"I do not paint," he said. "I am but a sculptor."

They walked slowly up the pebbled path, and through the bamboo grove, until they came to the little gate over which he had stepped.

"Now we have reached the wall," she said with childish lightness. "You are not so brave nowadays, I fancy, as to carry me across by force."

He vaulted to the other side without speaking, then stood a moment, looking back at her.

"Yet," she said, almost tremulously, "the wall is not so high or stone."

"It has the power to divide, O princess," he replied in a husky voice.

"Now you are at the other side, you are no longer Kamura Junzo," she said. "You have become changed from the little boy I once knew. You are cruel now—and—and—cold."

"And you," he said, "as far away and unattainable as the stars, O princess."

"Yet you are betrothed to one whom you called Masago," she said suddenly, and raised an almost appealing face to his. He looked into her eyes and did not speak.

"And am I not like this Masago?" she asked.

"You are like no one in all the world," he said, "save that sweet, lovely princess that even as a boy I sought to capture for—my own."

"You have not tried again," she said.

"The sun is in my eyes, O princess. I am afraid."

He turned abruptly from her and walked swiftly away toward the front of the palace.

"I have been dreaming," he said, passing his hand across his eyes, "and living in my dreams. O gods!"

Sado-ko looked after him, leaning over the railing of the gate watching until he disappeared. Then she turned and walked with dreamy step back through the bamboo grove. She turned toward a slender, pebbled path which she followed to a small lawn, in whose centre a stately statue, white and pure, was set. She stood in silence looking upon it,—a statue of the Prince Komatzu wrought by the hands of the artist-man. Suddenly she placed her arms about the statue's form and pressed her face against it. Her words were strangely like to his:—

"I have been dreaming, dreaming," she said, "and, O sweet Kuonnon, let me not awake!"

VII

The Picture by the Artist-man

The ladies persisted, though the artist was obdurate. He stood in their path directly before the covered picture on the foreign easel. His eyes wandered gravely over the various faces of his fair besiegers.

Said the Duchess Aoi, with her small chin raised and her long eyes at disdainful level:—

"Sir Artist, you invest a picture with the attributes of the original. Yet even the princess's most celestial person is not so sacred to our insignificant eyes. Why, then, her august picture?"

Junzo bowed only slightly to his interlocutor, and replied briefly:—

"The portrait is unfinished, Duchess Aoi."

"Unfinished! Well, and did we not gaze upon the statue of his Imperial Highness while yet it was unfinished?"

The artist did not move from his position.

"Ah, it is the honorable whim of the artist, ladies," said the little Countess Matsuka.

"Sir Artist, you are most cruel to the kind," chided a roguish young lady, who leaned against the Duchess Aoi.

"Yes, indeed," added another, "to permit a whim—an artist's foolish whim—to prevent our enjoyment of her Highness's picture."

"Confess," said Lady Fuji-no, who hitherto had remained quietly in the background, "that this is not the whim of an artist, but of—"

"The portrait is unfinished," repeated the artist, raising his voice.

"Shaka! You have been most painstaking, Sir Artist. The statue of the Prince Komatzu was completed in just half the space of time." It was the Duchess Aoi who spoke. To her the artist turned.

"Lady, bid me not again repeat, the portrait is unfinished," he said with a low, graceful bow.

Lady Fuji burst into merry laughter.

"Artist," she said, "the foreigners whom we emulate in some things declare that all women, royal or otherwise, have the prerogative to command, to insist."

Junzo's brows were slightly drawn together. He bowed without answering the smiling Fuji.

"And so," she continued, taking a step nearer to him, "I am going to look upon the picture, since you will not heed command, and even though—"

Her hand was upon the silken covering, which she had partly lifted. Junzo's hand fell upon hers like a vice. She did not, however, release the covering, but clutched at it beneath his fingers, her half-defiant, half-smiling eyes upon his face.

"Lady Fuji-no!" he cried, breathing heavily, "I must command—"

"Command!" she repeated haughtily; "and when, Sir Artist, did you acquire authority at court? By what right do you, a hired artist, dare to command a lady of the household of her Imperial Highness?"

She wrenched at the covering, and it began to slip from the top of the picture.

"In the name of Princess Sado-ko!" he cried.

The covering had slipped to the floor, and even the most impassive of the ladies had started back with little gasps of consternation. The canvas that faced them now was blank.

There was complete silence in the salon of the visiting artist. Then almost simultaneously all eyes were turned from that blank canvas to the face of the artist-man.

He stood there like one overtaken by a sudden tragedy. His face was white and drawn, his eyes, always large and dark, were widened now. His nostrils quivered, and his lips were dry. The very sight of his despair had a moving effect upon all, save the Lady Fuji-no, who began to laugh very softly. Thus she broke the silence. Her words were slow and cruel:—

"Of a truth, Sir Artist, the picture of her Imperial Highness is unfinished."

He did not speak. The lady leaned toward him, thrusting her face within the range of his vision.

"Is this the honorable portrait of our Princess Sado-ko, which she will make as exchange gift to her affianced, Prince Komatzu?" she asked.

The artist turned his face painfully aside. Then the Duchess Aoi spoke:—

"Artist," she said, "we most humble and insignificant ones copy the august fashions from her Highness. Pray you, paint my picture in just so fine a style."

There were hysterical tears in the voice of the little Countess Matsuka. She sought in vain to divert her more heartless companions.

ONOTO WATANNA

"I," she said, "would desire to be painted in a most gorgeous foreign gown."

"With the body showing?" inquired Madame Bara.

"Yes, the neck and the long arms. Why not?"

"Oh, ah, it is indecent!"

The artist stooped to the covering on the floor. He stood holding it in his hand, as though he knew not what to do.

"Oh, pray do not cover up the august likeness, artist," pleaded the Lady Fuji-no, with affected solicitude.

The Countess Matsuka raised her voice almost shrilly:—

"Ladies, do let us take a vote as to the decency of the barbarian gown."

But her suggestion was drowned in the hub-bub of gossip. The countess was met only with this reply:—

"Countess, upon what work was this artist-man engaged when he was closeted with Princess Sado-ko?"

The group about the picture grew closer still together. The question grew in size, and found a hundred answers.

"It is one that only the artist himself can solve," said Aoi, looking toward him obliquely.

"Oh, oh, was only the artist present?" protested Lady Fuji.

"And her Highness," said the Duchess Aoi, and bowed in mocking reverence at the name. "Do you not recall she said she would not have her ladies present at the sittings? When we dared to protest, in most humble wise, she frowned and commanded us to go, which we were forced to do."

The artist suddenly took a step forward and faced the ladies fairly. The color had returned to his face, and his eyes sparkled in defiant scorn at his small tormentors. His voice was raised to a clear pitch:—

"You make mistake, most noble ladies. You do injustice to the humble artist, to his work, and to her most exalted Highness." Here he bowed deeply and with reverence. "It is very true you do not now behold on this blank canvas the work of the many days of the artist. Yet that is not an unsolvable mystery. Shall the humble but honorable artist allow his work upon the portrait of her Serene Highness, the daughter of the sun-god, to remain in his most public salon for the chance and vulgar observation of the spiteful curious? Permit me to observe with proper respect and humility that no explanation of the substitution of the blank canvas is due. Further, ladies, you make a treasonable mistake when you declare the august sittings were unattended. Her Highness, upon all occasions when she deigned to permit me to paint her august picture, was both chaperoned and attended by the honorable maid, Onatsu-no."

A sudden little shriek broke from one of the ladies, at which all turned toward her and then followed the direction of her startled eyes. The next instant all this company of clattering-tongued ladies, whether in European dress or kimono, had fallen to their knees, and were touching the mats with their heads.

The Princess Sado-ko, attended by her maiden, Natsu-no, stepped slowly down from the slight eminence of the adjoining room, the shojis of which the pages drew behind her. There was no expression in the face of Sado-ko as she crossed the room, bowing her head with grace in response to the servile courtesies of her maids of honor. She made a slight motion with her hands, and there was a quick movement and rustling of the obedient ladies, moving toward the shoji that led without. One of them, more daring than the others, the Lady Fuji-no, paused by the veranda doors, and spoke with affected timidity:—

"May it please your Highness that we be permitted to remain to-day for this sitting?"

Sado-ko's eyes were above the head of her father's new favorite and her own maid of honor.

"Lady Fuji-no," she said, "I have spoken."

Fuji bowed herself down to the mats, then quietly joined those without.

VIII

A Sentimental Princess

Junzo turned his head from Sado-ko. He stood still as a statue, his head drooping, his hands clinched. She broke the strained silence with a command to her attendant.

"Natsu-no, pray draw apart the door at once. The atmosphere is thick with odor of our ladies. It has sickened the honorable artist."

He raised his head sharply. She had not heard, then! The maid pushed the shojis to either side, thus exposing the apartment to the full view of any without. This was a daily custom and precaution. No spying maid of honor might lurk about the balcony.

While the sliding doors remained open, neither the artist nor the princess spoke, but when a sufficient interval had elapsed and the doors had been drawn together again, the maid whispered a word of command to the guard outside, who silently took his station on the balcony. Then Sado-ko, turning slowly toward the artist, began to laugh in a strangely quivering, and subdued fashion. The sound of the soft laughter hurt the artist. He scarcely could command his words.

"Guileless princess, I pray you do not laugh!"

"Not laugh?" she repeated. "You are to-day a most unflattering artist. Was it only yesterday you said my laughter was as sweet as sweetest music of the sweetest birds?"

She passed her fan over her shoulder to the maid Natsu-no, who, whirling it open, fanned her gently. Sado-ko smiled reproachfully at Junzo, as she sat by a golden screen, near to a shoji through which the sinking sun pierced and slanted just above her head.

Junzo knelt on one knee a short distance from her. His face was sad and serious.

"Princess Sado-ko," he said, "you have not heard of a most lamentable happening."

"If," said she, still smiling, "you allude to the noisy chatter of my ladies, you are mistaken. I have heard."

He looked half unconsciously toward the now covered canvas. She followed his glance, and still she smiled.

"I have seen, too," she said.

He regarded her dumbly, marvelling at the trembling happiness which seemed to lurk within her eyes and about her small red lips.

"Come a pace nearer to me, if you please," she urged. His obedience brought him so close that he could have touched her. She put out a little hand toward him, and spoke his name.

"Junzo!" she said.

He scarcely dared to look at her. She said:—

"I pray you, look at me a space."

Their eyes met fully now, and then he saw that despite the smile within them, hers were shining with undropped tears. In an agony of feeling he turned from her. He heard her tremulous voice, thrilling now with that strange laughing quality but accentuating the pleading underneath.

"Do not even the birds chatter? Permit my ladies the same pastime."

"It is of you I think," he said huskily.

"That is all very well. I—I would not have you think of—of another," she replied.

"Princess, the gossip of the ladies does injury to your sweet name."

"If that were so," she said, "there would be no such name as Sado-ko left in the world. Do you not know that I am the most unpopular princess in Japan?"

"But this late matter, princess, is not merely female resentment at your refusal to accept the Western mode of life within your household. But this new slan—"

"Do not speak the word," she said quietly.

She took her fan from Natsu-no, and arising crossed the room until she stood before the easel. Pensively she looked at the covered canvas. Junzo had followed her and now stood by her side. There was deep emotion in his voice:—

"Princess, will it please you to sit to-day?"

She turned to raise her eyes to his.

"But," she said, "you do not paint upon the canvas. You have told me so."

"I am a sculptor, but I have also attempted the other—"

She interrupted him.

"It would hurt your fame," she said. "It cannot be."

"And what does it matter whether I have fame or not?"

"Artist, it was not for that work I bade you stay," she said.

"But it was thought so by the others, princess."

"I—I had a desire to learn more of—of Kamakura—of people there—and so I begged you to remain."

"You did command," he said in a low voice.

"No," raising her eyes appealingly, "say that I did beseech you."

"You did command," he repeated.

"Well, have it so. I commanded and you obeyed. It was the reason of your staying. Why suggest employment now?"

"To spare the name of the most noble princess in the realm."

She held her little head proudly.

"Who is it that slanders Sado-ko," she asked scornfully, and then quickly answered herself. "A few small biting insects, who but sting, not kill, Sir Artist."

He turned away from her and stood by the garden shoji, from whence he stared moodily without. She followed him with softest step.

"I pray you, do not look without. The sky is gray. The sun is fading."

She put her hand upon his arm with timid touch. He turned with sudden impulse, and seized it in both his own.

"The sun, O princess, is within," he cried, "and, O sweet Sado-ko, it is too dazzling bright for such as I to gaze upon."

When he would have dropped her hand, she held it within his own. Her face filled him with a vague longing. He trembled at her touch. He felt the wavering of her head toward him, then its touch against his arm, where now it rested. A remnant of reason remaining within him, he sought to draw apart from her.

"Do not—do not so," she cried, clinging to him.

"My touch profanes you, Sado-ko," he whispered hoarsely.

"It does not," she denied, with tears in her appealing voice. "Pray you, do not draw your arm away."

"Princess!"

"I do command again," she said. After that he did not speak.

Suddenly the silent, immovable figure of the maid seemed to take upon itself the first signs of life. She arose and moved toward her mistress. At a respectful distance she spoke.

"Noble princess!" she said.

Sado-ko, still holding the arm of her lover close about her, turned toward the maid.

"What is your honorable desire, maiden?"

"The chamber darkens, O princess. Will your Highness deign to permit the honorable light?"

"I am quite satisfied," said Sado-ko, and rested her head contentedly against the artist's arm. The maid did not move.

"Will not the noble princess permit her evening meal?" she asked in trembling tones.

"I am not hungry," said the Princess Sado-ko. She smiled up at her lover's now adoring face.

"Princess, the hour of—"

Sado-ko turned toward the maid with the first show of impatience.

"Pray return to your seat, Natsu-no," she said, "and when I need your service, I will so advise you."

Without replying, Natsu-no slowly moved to her seat; but she kept her face toward those two figures now silhouetted in the twilight of the room.

"You still are uneasy?" asked the Princess Sado-ko. "Do you not like the touch of me?"

"It makes me faint with ecstasy," he said. "Yet, Sado-ko, I am fearful."

"Oh, be not fearful," she said.

"On my knees I could adore you, but—"

"But? You do not finish."

"Princess!"

"Do not call me princess. Forget for but a little while that I am such. I, too, would forget, my Junzo."

"I must remember for us both," he said. "My honor—O sweet Sado-ko—thy honor—"

"Sado-ko is ill with honor," she replied. "Give me for a change a little of that simple love I have not had since my august grandmother died."

"O innocent princess!"

She laughed softly.

"Junzo, they say that I was born without a heart, that because I was the child of gods I could not love as mortals do. Could you not tell them otherwise, my Junzo?"

The maid was weeping in the darkened room, her sobs clearly audible. They heard her crawling on her knees across the room, and then the soft thud of her prostration before the little shrine. Then came the mumbling words of her prayer:—

"Hear thou the prayer of the most humble one, O mighty Kuonnon. Save thou the soul of thy innocent descendant, she who—"

Sado-ko dropped the arm of her lover and started toward the maid.

"Natsu-no!" she cried out sharply, as the drone of the woman's prayer ended, "for whom do you pray?"

The maid put her head at the princess's feet.

"For you, O beloved mistress, I pray that the gods will save you from this artist-man."

The princess spurned her with her little foot.

"If you make such foolish prayers, the gods may hear you," she cried. "If they should grant your prayers and take him from me, why, I should be bereft of—Oh-h—"

She made a passionate movement toward the shrine, as though she would destroy it, but strong hands drew her away.

"Do not, Sado-ko, offend the gods! Do not, for my sake!"

She put her hands upon his shoulders and wept against his breast.

IX

Moon Tryst

Like a large lighted lantern the palace Komatzu appeared in the night. Its transparent shojis revealed the lights within. The sound of soft tinkling music was constantly heard, an accompaniment to the ceaseless murmuring of voices. Ever and anon there was the sound of silvery laughter, and also the soft glide and patter of moving footsteps.

From the garden without one could see the strange flitting and moving of the figures within, for the court of Japan was enjoying the latest of Western novelties,—the dance. A square-bearded German had found a place as leader of the Japanese orchestra, and now a strange medley of dance music was being wrung from the instruments. The weird tinkling of the geishas' instruments floating out from a garden booth close at hand, added discord to the odd orchestra of the palace. Yet the gentlemen and ladies of the court glided and tripped back and forth within, and thought that they were dancing quite in the style of the fashionable Westerners.

But while all was gay and brilliant in the new ball-room of the palace Komatzu, that wing of the palace reserved for the Princess Sado-ko was in blackness.

Sado-ko stood alone in her darkened chamber. She had dismissed her personal attendant, Natsu-no, though the latter crouched by the inner shoji, her eye peering into the adjoining room, watching and guarding her mistress.

It had not been difficult for Sado-ko to retire from the ball, when the dancing had begun, for her aversion to all such modern pastimes was well known. She alone of all that company had appeared in the simple though exquisite garb of her country. In a robe of ancient style, soft flowing, Sado-ko had never appeared to better advantage among the ladies of the court, all of whom affected the European style of gown, which ill became them.

Now in her chamber alone, Sado-ko watched by her shoji. When first she took her stand, all was black without. No moon had yet arisen to silver her own gardens and tell her that it was time. It was a long interval while she stood there, a statue of patience.

ONOTO WATANNA

Gradually the darkness without became mellowed, and slowly and softly the tall bamboos and pines became silhouetted against the sky. One small hand hidden in the folds of her kimono was lifted. She pushed the shoji a small way apart,—only enough room for her straining eyes to see clearer without.

It was a white and wistful face she turned appealingly to the skies. Then that first soft light reflected in her eyes, and sighing with relief that her waiting now was over, she pushed the sliding doors still farther apart and then stepped outside. She paused upon her balcony, to look about her with some fear. There was no sound or stir. Very distant and far away sounded the music of the palace Komatzu.

With another glance of assurance at the moon floating up from the hills and trees, she lifted her gown. Down into the garden the princess stepped.

Almost at the same instant the maiden Natsu-no cautiously pushed back the shoji the princess had forgotten to close, and keeping some distance behind, followed her mistress with stealing step.

Meanwhile the Lady Fuji-no had slipped breathlessly from the arms of her partner, and condemning the atmosphere of the room had sought the wide verandas. Save for the silent and melancholy figure of the artist the verandas were deserted. He stood by the steps leading to the gardens, his arms folded across his breast, his head partly upraised as though he watched the skies. At the light touch of the Lady Fuji's hand he started violently, forgetting his manners in so far as to draw his sleeve quickly away from her clasp. Her face was in shadow, for it was dark about them. Only the first glimmer of the moon had yet appeared. Junzo knew that she was smiling mockingly.

"You watch the stars, Sir Artist?" she asked sweetly.

"Yes," he replied, without moving.

"So! They are very beautiful to-night."

"Honorably so," he replied simply.

"Yet how insignificant will they appear shortly when their august queen shall arise to dim their little lustre."

"It is so," he agreed gravely; "the august moon is queen of the night."

"You watch for the queen, Sir Artist?"

He turned and looked at her curiously.

"And you, my lady?"

"I, too," she rejoined.

He moved restlessly, and even in the dim light her watching eyes saw the uneasiness in his face.

"Let us watch for her together, artist."

"I would not take you from your pleasures within, my lady."

"Nay, the pleasures without overshadow those within."

Again she saw the anxious glance upward toward the hills, and in the darkness the Lady Fuji smiled behind her opened fan. Junzo moved downward a few steps; he paused irresolutely.

"The garden is fragrant, Lady Fuji-no. I would enjoy it for a little while."

"And I," said she, and went a step downward.

"But the air is chill, my lady."

"Balmy sweet, Sir Artist."

"Lady, your august neck and arms are bare to the night," he said.

She drew herself up slightly, and looked down a space at her low gown.

"The musicians and the geishas in the booths," he said, "would dishonor you with their rude glances."

Without replying she clapped, her hands. A page came at the signal.

"A wrap, if you please," she ordered.

Junzo, now at the foot of the steps, stirred uneasily. The moon was in full view. The sight for which he had watched so anxiously filled him now only with agitation and despair. He thought of one waiting in the darkness of the private gardens beyond. Anxiety rendered him reckless. He bowed deeply to the Lady Fuji-no.

"Lady, I implore your august pardon, but the night has claims upon my desires. I wish to wander with it alone."

She stooped down toward him. Her words, though whispered, were perfectly clear.

"You have a moon tryst, Sir Artist. Oh, beware!"

He turned about sharply and faced her.

"The Moon," she said,—"you will become her plaything, artist. Be cautioned!"

Uncertain and irresolute he stood a moment, then turned upon his heel and swiftly strode down along the path, disappearing into the shadows of the trees.

Sado-ko wandered through the dewy gardens, beneath the drooping bamboos and the towering pines. Her little feet were swift and willing, as she hastened along with beating heart; but when she approached the end of the grove, though there was light beyond, she could not see even the shadow of that one who was to have kept the tryst with her. Her steps faltered; she went less swiftly.

"The moon is late," she said. And then, "It was the light of the stars I saw."

She walked so slowly now, that her little feet became entangled in her flowing gown, which she had absently let fall to the ground. The end of the grove was now reached. She could see the bright silver light without.

In the shadow of the last bamboo the princess stood and trembled. She did not need to peer into the distance, for all was clear outside the bamboo grove, as far off as the dividing line of the boxwood shrub and the small white gate. How long she stood in silent waiting she could not have told. Every passing summer breeze made her shiver. Once she raised her hand to her face, and something wet was wiped away.

"'Tis but the dew upon my face," she said, but her own trembling voice broke the spell of anguished waiting. At the foot of the drooping bamboo she slipped to the earth, and crouched beneath the shadow, deaf now to all sounds, save her own inward heart cries and the tears which even she could not command to cease.

Yet after only a little while, one appeared at the bamboo gate, vaulted quickly over it, and came with running feet on toward the grove. A moment later, Sado-ko was in the arms of her lover.

"Oh, is it you—you!" she said through her sighs, "at last. Oh, at last you have come!"

"It is I, sweet Sado-ko."

"So late!" she said, her breath caught by her sobs.

"Yes, late," he said, "but it was not the fault of Junzo."

"I kept the tryst," she said, "and waited long for the moon to rise—and then—then you did not come, and I—and then I wept."

She turned her face toward a moonbeam streaming through the grove that he might see the glistening tears.

"Sado-ko!" he cried in an agony, "oh, that I should cause you pain—I who would sell my very soul to save you from a tear."

She had recovered somewhat of her natural calm, and for a moment her old bright self shone out.

"Nay, then, and what is a little tear? So slight a thing—see, I will wipe it away with the sleeve of my Junzo."

"My lotos maiden! O Sado-ko, I have made enemies for you here in this very palace."

"But I am stronger than the enemies, my Junzo. Indeed, I can afford to laugh at them."

"One—the Lady Fuji, do not trust her, I beseech you, Sado-ko."

"She would become wife to my father," said Sado-ko, with quiet scorn, "yet her power is small and her hope vain."

"She tried to prevent my coming here to-night. I fear she has suspected our tryst."

"Lady Fuji-no is wise. Were I to marry soon the Prince Komatzu, her fortunes would change. She would possibly be out of service, and knows or thinks my father would befriend her."

"There are still others. I fear the Duchess Aoi has no love for you or me."

"She has love for only one besides herself,—the Prince Komatzu. She could much better herself in his graces, could she betray Sado-ko in some base act."

"And baseness is not possible in Sado-ko," he said.

Her little hands moved softly across his breast and upon his arms.

"You are truly here, my Junzo," she said, "I do not dream."

"Hark, something is stirring close by!"

"The wind," she said. "Pray you, be not fearful of the wind."

"It seemed a sound more human-like, as of one who crept along the grove."

"Perchance a deer. The parks are fully stocked, and many wander hither to my own private gardens."

He raised her face upward between his hands, within which he framed it.

"Listen, Sado-ko. Do you forget that we made this tryst to-night for a sad purpose?"

"I have forgotten," she murmured; and added in so soft a voice, "I would forget, dear Junzo."

"O Sado-ko, it is sweet to be together, but sadder still than sweet, for this must be the last time."

She shook her head.

"No, no," she said. "I will not let you go."

"I must go," he said sadly.

"I will command you to stay," she said.

"I cannot longer stay. To-morrow—"

"I will implore you, then. Go not away from me, dear Junzo!"

"Have you forgotten that our tryst to-night was made to say our most sad sayonaras?"

ONOTO WATANNA

She lifted his sleeve, and held it close against her face.

"No, no—leave me not!"

His voice was husky.

"Why, Sado-ko, to-morrow there will be an exodus from the palace. I could not stay, even if I would. Does not the Prince Komatzu journey back to Tokyo?"

"And you—you, too, will go with us," she said.

"I?"

"I have myself asked this favor of my cousin."

"You asked his Highness—"

"Yes. I bade him ask you to accompany us, so you might have the honorable commission to paint the pictures of the ladies of the court."

"Paint the pictures—" repeated Junzo, stupidly.

"Yes, that will be the good excuse. Yet you must not do so. No, I would not have you work upon another's beauty."

"I cannot go," he said, raising his voice. "It is impossible. I must return."

She started back, her hands above her heart.

"I understand," she said. "You will return to—"

He seized her hands with impulsive passion.

"My father bids me return. Can I refuse?" he cried.

"Oh, go not back!" she said, with tears in her pleading voice.

"I must return. I am but a son. Does not a son owe his first obedience in life to his father?"

"It is an ancient fancy," she said, "and these moderns are more wise. They say a man must give his first thought to"—her voice dropped and broke—"his wife!"

She drew her hands from his, and covered her face with them. While yet her face was hidden in them she spoke:—

"You will make *her*—your wife?"

He could not answer. Her hands dropped from her face to clinch now at her sides.

"Answer, if you please!" she said.

"It is my father's command," he said in a low voice.

"Your father's command is greater, then, than mine?" she demanded with fierceness.

"O Sado-ko, do you not perceive my despair?"

"But why should you despair?—you who are to marry Masago!"

"Sado-ko!" he cried with piercing reproach, "all the gods of heaven have forbidden me union with you. Tell me what other course is left."

"Oh, leave me not!" said Sado-ko.

"Even if I would, I could not stay. Your august relatives would hastily learn the truth, and then—"

They heard a slight cry within the darkness of the grove. Then something white flashed by them into the open.

"Look!" cried Sado-ko, clutching his sleeve. "Oh, see!"

By the white bamboo gate two figures were outlined,—a man and woman. And in the clear moonlight the lovers recognized them as the Prince Komatzu and the Duchess Aoi. But the maid Onatsu-no, who had rushed by them so swiftly through the grove, came up toward these two by the gate, and prostrated herself before them.

"Quick!" cried Sado-ko. "They have not seen us yet. Natsu-no will speak to them. Meanwhile run with all the speed your love for me can lend, back through the grove. Hide among the shadows of the trees until the prince and I shall pass. Then return along the grove."

He lingered, seeming averse to hiding; but she urged him, pushing him with her own hands.

"There—go—for my sake—my sake—do this thing for me!" she urged disjointedly.

He stooped and drew her hands close to his face, and for a moment looked deep into her eyes.

"Sayonara!" he whispered. "It is forever."

"Sayonara!" she repeated, and sobbed over the word, "for a little time," she said.

X

Cousin Komatzu

Sado-ko stepped from out the shadow of the bamboo grove into the moon-lit path, and seemingly pensive, made her way toward the two at the gate. She paused before them silently for a moment, then made a gesture of dismissal to the maid Natsu-no, who ceased her excited apologies for having interrupted them, through sudden fright at their appearance.

"Cousin," said the princess to Komatzu, ignoring altogether the Duchess Aoi, "your sudden appearance at my gate has frightened both my maid and me, who in our solitary evening rambles not often meet with visitors."

Komatzu answered:—

"The Duchess Aoi and the Lady Moon both beguiled me into a like garden wandering. We came but by chance to your august gate."

"But will you not step inside?" asked Sado-ko. "Pray, cousin, will you not walk with me?" she sweetly urged.

Glad to accompany his cousin, the prince, softly clapping his hands, ordered an attendant to unfasten the gate. Aoi was about to follow him to the other side, when stopped by the voice of the princess. "We do not need your further service to-night," she said.

The mortified duchess bowed to the earth, and slowly moved away.

When she was gone and the Princess Sado-ko should have breathed more freely, a reaction came. She clung with sudden faintness to the waiting-maid, Natsu-no.

"Cousin, you are ill!" cried the dismayed Komatzu.

She tried to laugh, but her voice was shaking and her words piteous.

"I but stumbled on my gown, Sir Cousin."

She raised herself, lifting the kimono a little upward from the ground.

"It is the punishment of vanity," she continued in a somewhat weary voice. "I was not ready to part with my fair gown, Komatzu. It is of ancient style and very long and cumbersome."

"But the embodiment of grace and beauty," said Komatzu, gallantly.

She pursued this light conversation, in hope of diverting him as they passed on their way through the grove.

"What, Cousin Komatzu, you praise an Oriental gown,—you who are so much a modern!"

He glanced down smilingly at his evening dress, black, immaculate, and foreign.

"The honorable gown, fair cousin, is truly exquisite; still, I confess I do prefer the foreign style, and would that you did also."

"But I should suffocate did I enclose my little frame in so honorably tight a garb," she protested, and at the same moment she glanced about fearfully. Komatzu seemed to perceive something of her uneasiness, for he, too, cast a keen look about them.

In nervousness she began to speak again, for somewhere close at hand she heard a stir which set her heart to violent beating.

"My ladies beg permission to deck your statue with august flowers, cousin, and—Ah-h!"

She paused. Was it fancy only, or did she see a face staring out at her from the dense foliage hard by?

"I protest," said Komatzu, stopping short in his walk, "that you, fair cousin, are ill. You are not your familiar self to-night."

Her fingers clutched his arm as she drew him again along the path.

"No, no, no," she denied, "I am quite well! Do not linger here, I pray you, Cousin Komatzu."

He frowned, glancing out with brows drawn.

"I was thinking it an ideal spot for loitering, princess."

"'Tis dark," said Sado-ko, still hastening blindly on.

"The moonlight is on all sides, cousin, and pierces through the thin bamboos. And look upward—see how clear and beautiful the star-lit sky above us."

Again he paused in admiring contemplation of the night.

"The night is chill, Sir Cousin, and the grove is damp," she said.

"Why, no—" he began again in protest, when the maid behind interrupted. She wrapped a cape about the shoulders of her mistress, and spoke in soothing tones:—

"Noble princess, the humble one was witness of your shivering just now. Permit me then to serve you."

Still the Prince Komatzu hesitated. Suddenly Sado-ko thrust into his her own small hands.

"Cousin, feel how cold my hands are. Will you not warm them with yours?" she said.

He held them doubtfully a moment, then chafed them with his own, while she moved onward.

Once outside the grove, a great breath, a sigh, escaped the agitated Sado-ko. Then suddenly she began to laugh in a strange, mirthless fashion, as one who laughs through tears. Her cousin stood in silence, sombrely regarding her. When she had ceased, he asked:—

"Why did you laugh so suddenly just now, princess?"

"A thought came to my honorable little brain, Komatzu. I fancied that you had learned that I would keep a tryst to-night."

He did not move, and she continued with hysterical rapidity.

"And by your face I know my thought was true. Did not the Duchess Aoi bring you to my gate for the purpose of—a spy?"

"We came by chance," he answered gravely.

"Yes, chance dictated by your beguiling guide, good cousin. Is it not so?"

"The Duchess Aoi spoke with indignation of the tales of others, Sado-ko."

Again the princess laughed in that weird way.

"It is a habit of my sex, Komatzu, to slander one in just that wise, veiling beneath choice, soft, indignant words against others their own subtle design of defamation."

"Cousin, who would dare defame your name to me?"

"Oh, any fair and clever lady of the court, Komatzu. Come, cousin, were you not informed that I would keep a tryst to-night?"

"With whom could Princess Sado-ko keep tryst?" he asked.

She shrugged her shoulders recklessly.

"With whom, Komatzu? The stars, the moon, the night,—perchance, a lover."

"You laugh at me, fair cousin."

"Permit me, then, to weep." She clasped her face with both her hands, but she did not feign tears: they came too readily.

"Cousin," said Komatzu, solemnly, "will you make an exchange gift with me for my august statue?"

She raised her face defiantly.

"And why should you and I make exchange gifts, Komatzu? We are not affianced."

"Are we not?" he asked sternly.

"No, save for the gossip of the court and popular fancy. Yet his Majesty has not betrothed us, and I am both his niece and ward."

"He will betroth us," said Komatsu, with gloomy assurance, "for all his ministers are in favor of the union."

"We will abide the time, Komatsu, when his Majesty sanctions it. Meanwhile we are but cousins."

"Sado-ko, give me that picture of you painted by the artist."

She turned her face away. Her nervous hands were clasped.

"When we are betrothed," she said.

"Sado-ko, you know I am your lover."

"So it is said."

"Who but a lover should possess this likeness of your Highness?"

"You are not my lover—yet."

"I will be so," said Komatsu. "Give me, I repeat, the portrait of your Highness."

She turned toward him, like one brought suddenly to desperate bay.

"Why require this of me? You have already learned there is no such picture."

"What, you admit it!"

"I admit it," she returned quietly now.

He changed his haughty tone to one wherein there was more sorrow than anger.

"Tell me this, Cousin Sado-ko, why did the artist remain, and upon what work was he engaged when closeted with you?"

"He did not work, Komatsu. He but spoke to me—and I to him. He would have gone, but I commanded him to stay. There was no option for the man. He could not paint. I knew this all the time—yet—still—I bade him stay."

"Why, Princess Sado-ko?"

"For many reasons. I wished to know of other lives. The shallow, shameless ones of those about me enervated my body and my soul. I wished to learn of others in the world, fresh, cleaner, cousin."

"Sado-ko, I fear you were misjudged. I fathom now your reasons. Just one more bit of eccentricity so natural to our cousin."

"And so he stayed," she said, her voice now slow and almost absent in its tone, as though she were recalling incidents in some far past. "He stayed, as I commanded. He told me of *his* world,—the great world without, Komatsu, where men were men, not puppets. He had travelled much, Komatsu,—fairly round the world, it seems; and though he dressed not in the garb of the barbarian, he knew more of them than the whole of this affected court."

"He spoke of the foreign world?"

"That and of other things."

"Other things?"

Her voice dragged slowly over the word as she spoke in answer.

"Masago!" she murmured in a low voice.

"And who, I pray, is this Masago?"

"Masago," she repeated; and then again, "Masago. Do you like the sound of the name, cousin?"

"It has a fair but common sound. The 'morning glory' is esteemed. It is, in truth, a pretty name."

"But not so sweet as—Sado-ko. Pray you, say so, cousin."

"Why, no; not so sweet, so rare, so royal. Who but a princess might carry such a name as that? Does not the 'ko' mean 'royal' and 'Sado,' sweetest name for maiden, 'chastity'?"

Her restless hands unclasped. She raised a trembling face.

"Komatzu, I would exchange that royal name for the simple one—Masago."

"Princess!"

"I weary of that title, cousin."

"Who is this Masago?"

"A simple, happy maid, Komatzu. She is the daughter of a late countryman of Echizen, and now a famous merchant of Tokyo."

"What is his name?"

"Yamada Kwacho. Ah, I see you start, Komatzu. You, too, it seems, have heard the story?"

"And you?"

"And I. But not until he came to Komatzu."

"He?—this artist-fellow told you of your father?"

"No. His coming simply widened the lips of the ever open mouths of my sweet maids of honor. By a female chance of listening, a weakness common to our race and sex, Komatzu, I heard the tale retold."

Komatzu made a gesture of impatience.

"Cousin, I apologize for the vile gossip with which my palace seems infected."

"Oh, spare your august tongue, Komatzu. 'Twas my own maids who spoke."

"And this Masago? I do not altogether understand. She is a daughter of Yamada Kwacho?"

"A daughter of his wife, Komatzu."

The subtle meaning of her words was not lost upon the prince. He frowned.

"What relation does this Masago bear to this artist-man?" he asked.

Sado-ko looked up at him in the now fading moonlight, but did not answer. The expression of her face was strange. She turned suddenly, and moved with slow and almost dreamy step toward her rooms, Komatzu following at her side, awaiting her reply.

Sado-ko paused on the steps, and then she answered in the faintest voice:—

"Masago is his bride to be, Komatzu."

In the opening of the shoji she paused a space, looking up at the sky.

"The moon is gone," she said. Her cousin did not know whether to him she breathed farewell, or to the moon, for she said:—

"Sayonara!" and then, "O moon!"

XI

A Mirror and a Photograph

W hy do you weep?" asked Sado-ko.

"O noble princess," stammered Natsu-no, "I would that you could weep with me."

"Maiden, I have shed all the tears that I can spare."

The princess arose, to stand for a moment in indecisive silence. For the space of an hour, princess and maid had sat in silence in the darkened chamber.

"Bring a light, maiden," said the princess, "but do not awaken the pages. Serve me to-night alone."

The maid bowed obediently. From the adjoining room she brought a lighted andon, and hesitatingly set it on the floor, looking wistfully meanwhile at her mistress.

"Go now to your deserved sleep, good maid," said Sado-ko, indicating the chamber beyond.

"And you, sweet mistress?"

"I will not need your further offices to-night."

"Pray you, dear princess, permit the humble one to robe you for the night."

"I have spoken, Natsu-no."

The maid turned unwillingly, and pushing slowly aside the sliding doors, disappeared within.

Sado-ko lifted the andon and carried it across the room. Holding it in her hand on a level with her eyes, she examined the wall, and found a sliding panel. This she pushed aside, drew from out the recess an ancient rounded mirror. She set the andon on the floor, and then lay down beside it. Thus, lying sidewise, the light at her head, she could hold the mirror before her face, and see the reflection within.

For a long time she seemed to study the features in silence. Then sitting up again she drew from her sleeve a piece of modern cardboard, such as foreign photographers use. This she also held to the andon light.

The face which had looked at her from the mirror now stared up at her with cold, inscrutable eyes from the photograph in her hand. Yet there was a subtle difference in the expression of the face of the mirror, and that of the card, for the one was wistful, soul-eyed, and appealing, while the other was of that perfect waxen type of woman whose soul one dreams of but seldom sees. The one was the face of the statue, the other that of the statue come to life.

Suddenly Sado-ko set picture and mirror aside, and arising, crossed to the sliding doors. These she pushed apart.

"Maiden!" she called into the room, "Natsu-no."

The tired waiting-woman was asleep by the dividing shoji. She awoke with a start and hastened to her mistress, murmuring her apologies.

"Come hither," said the princess. "I have something here to show you."

She led the maid by the sleeve to the andon upon the floor. Together they crouched beside it, while Sado-ko gave the picture into the hands of Natsu-no. The maid stared at it in some bewilderment, then held it further in the light.

"Tell me, maiden, who is this?"

Still the maid held it in the light. Her eyes widened, then suddenly she bent her head before the pictured face, next to the floor.

"Who is this?" repeated Sado-ko.

"You, sweet mistress," said the maid,—"a most bewitching honorable likeness of your Highness."

"You are sure?" asked Sado-ko, smiling strangely.

"As sure as that the night is night," declared the maid, again regarding the picture.

"Maiden, does a princess wear flowers in her hair? See, there is the bara (rose) to either side on this girl's head."

Natsu-no started.

"No, no, exalted one."

"Did ever princess wear such a gown as this, my maiden?"

"Oh, princess!" The woman appeared shaken with a sudden terror.

"Do not drop the picture, if you please," said Sado-ko, "but look at it again. Observe the knotted fashion of the obi, Natsu-no. Quite in the style of a geisha, is it not?—or rather the poor imitation of some simple maid who would copy the style from the pleasure women."

The maid dropped the picture as though a thing unclean. At that motion the princess still smiled, but more inscrutably.

"Oh, noble princess, what evil one did dare to put your Highness's face upon such a picture? It is a national disgrace."

Reflectively Sado-ko looked at the picture.

"Perhaps it was the gods, O Natsu-no," she said, as silently she put the picture in her sleeve.

She arose, regarding her maid's emotion.

"Come," she ordered, "undress me for the night, good maiden, for I am very tired, and to-morrow—to-morrow we must go upon a journey."

"To Tokyo," said Natsu, "with the noble Prince Komatzu's suite, and oh, sweet mistress, life will have a happier aspect when we leave this melancholy place."

Lifting her hands to her head, Sado-ko withdrew the long jewelled pins. Her hair fell in midnight glory to her knees.

Kneeling by her, the maid tied her hair back, a very old-fashioned mode which the ladies in her grandmother's youth were fond of following when retiring, and to which the Princess Sado-ko had faithfully adhered.

"Does the honorable cortège leave before noon?" asked the maid.

"Yes."

"And all the kuge (court nobles) and the ladies, also, go?"

"Yes."

"Then I must haste. The sky already lightens. The night is past. When will my mistress sleep?"

"There is much time for us to sleep to-morrow. We do not accompany Prince Komatzu's train," said Sado-ko in a low voice, as though she spoke half to herself.

The maid paused in her arrangement of her mistress's couch, and, kneeling, stared at her.

"Noble princess, did you not just now speak of a journey?" she asked, with evident agitation.

"Yes," said the princess, wearily; "to-morrow we also will make a journey, but—we go alone! Pray you, hurry with my bed, Natsu-no."

Without speaking the maid drew the robe about the princess, now upon the couch. Then she spread her own quilt-mattress at the feet of her mistress.

"Good night, kind maid," said Sado-ko, and closed her eyes.

"Princess!" cried the maid, in a choked voice, "forgive the insignificant one, but whither do we journey to-morrow?"

"To Kamakura," said the princess, in a dragging voice; she was tired now. "We will go for a little while—just a little while, Natsu-no, to the castle Aoyama."

The maid was speechless. When she found her tongue, its faltering sentences betrayed her agitation.

"Princess—the artist-man—"

"Has gone to-night. Take peace, restless maid. Good night."

"But whither, Lady Princess, whither went the artist-man?"

"I bid you speak no more. Good night."

THE HOUSE PARTY OF THE Prince Komatzu ended the following day. A special train carried the exalted ones back to Tokyo, whither they went at once to the palace Nijo, for there Komatzu always made his home in Tokyo, with his cousin, the Prince of Nijo.

There was much gossip and idle conjecture in the party as to the caprice of the Princess Sado-ko. At the last moment she had despatched word to Komatzu, saying that she would not travel in the unholy barbarian train, but preferred to proceed leisurely to Tokyo in the old-fashioned but honorable mode of travel,—by kago or norimono. Should the journey prove too tiresome for her strength, she would stop a little while in Kamakura, at the castle Aoyama, and there it was possible she might spend a day or two in maidenly retirement. She desired, however, that her suite should not await her, but proceed with the train to Tokyo. She did not wish to deprive them of the enjoyment (to them) of the peculiar foreign method of travel, and would need only her personal attendants,—eight men retainers, whom she still termed "samurai," the chaperon, old Madame Bara, and her waiting-woman, Natsu-no.

XII

Mists of Kamakura

There were marsh lands and boggy rice-fields in the valley country along the Hayama, and during the season of White Dew (end of August) the river was low and scarcely seemed to stir.

In the early morning a white mist arose from it, eerily enshrouding the land like a veil of gauze, evaporating, and disappearing slowly. Sometimes, too, at night heavy fogs rose up even to the hills and obscured all sight of land. Oftentimes the traveller, even the native, lost his way. Tales were told of the smiling, languorous river, whose beauty, siren-like, lured her victims to destruction.

Even the villagers, whose homes nestled so cosily in the fragrant valleys, did not venture out on foggy nights in the direction of the river, unless attended by the Hayama guide, Oka, who boasted he could find his way blind-folded among the familiar paths of Kamakura, even to the very water's edge.

Almost beyond sight of the village, above the heads of the sloping hills, the lordly castle Aoyama looked over the mists of the valley at Fuji in the sky distance.

It was five o'clock in the afternoon. A young girl sat by an open shoji, motionless and silent, staring up at the ghost-like hills. The descending mists told her that long before the darkness came all sight of the spot upon which she gazed would be obliterated. She lingered on in melancholy discontent, her chin upon her hand, her embroidery frame idle at her side.

Beyond a few servants of the household no one was at home save Masago. She knew that her thoughts and meditations would be free from interruption, and so she gave herself up to them unreservedly, with inward passion.

The Yamada house was situated on a rising eminence. From the maiden Masago's casement the golden peaks of the palace Aoyama were visible. It was upon these points that the young girl fixed her eyes with a vague expression of suffering, wistfulness, and yearning.

What were the thoughts of Masago, fresh from the training of a modern and fashionable school in the old capital of Kyoto? The dreams that had stirred the apathetic mind of Ohano's daughter into vague discontent had not been removed by the months of schooling, but were more definite, and therefore more painful.

In Masago's hands was the same picture of the martial prince-hero which she had once cut from a Chinese magazine, and which since then she had never ceased to adore. Always this shining prince was entangled in her other dreams. Hands and eyes now both were fixed upon her heart's desire.

To her the stately palace Aoyama bespoke that other world, intoxicating, ecstatic, desirable, upon the very edge of which she might not even cling,—she who had been born to it. The innate craving of the Prince of Nijo for the sensations of the upper world ate at the very heart of the daughter of Ohano. To her, life in this world was the most desirable thing on earth; it must satisfy every craving of the mind and heart, and in it, Masago knew, belonged her hero-prince. She was not the only humble maiden of Japan who secretly worshipped the nation's martial hero, but possibly her love for him was a more personal thing, because deep in the girl's consciousness always was the knowledge that she might have been worthy of him, had not the irony of fate willed it otherwise, and set her here, a thing apart from him, caged and guarded by such surroundings,—she, a daughter of the Prince of Nijo and blood niece to the Emperor of Japan.

Only three days before the royal fiancée of her hero had arrived at the palace Aoyama. There, sheltered, nurtured, and watched over, the favored daughter of the gods, report had said, had gone into maiden retirement pending her nuptials. Masago thought of her with feelings akin to hatred, impotent and desperate, but ceaseless. She knew that on the morrow this Princess Sado-ko would resume her journey to the city of Tokyo. Soon she would have joined her lover, her future husband, in the capital.

"To-night," said Masago, moistening her dry lips, "she will think of him, and all night long,—it is her privilege. While I—I, too, will think of him—"

She hid her miserable face within her hands and rocked herself to and fro, thinking of what the morrow must do for her. She knew that Kamura Junzo, her affianced, had returned to Kamakura. Had not her parents gone this very day to attend a family council? Masago had been glad of the creeping fog which slowly spread across the land, as she knew this would prevent her parents' return that night. She had craved for these moments of maiden privacy. Soon they must cease when she had been given to this man for wife.

A servant brought Masago her evening tea, which the girl mechanically drank as she nibbled at the crisp rice cakes. She did not speak to the attendant while she dined, but continued to stare before her through the opened shoji. When she had finished, she clapped her hands, at which signal the tray was carried away.

The shadow and the fog intermingled, darkening the sky without and deepening the twilight gloom of the room. A little later the servant returned, bringing a lighted andon, which she set significantly by the silent girl. Then Masago stirred from her abstraction. She saw the eyes of the servant upon the picture in her hand. On a sudden, savage impulse she leaped to her feet and fairly sprung upon the woman, clutching her by the shoulders.

"Always look! Always see! Foolwoman!" she said in a whisper which was yet a cry.

The woman shook the hands from her shoulders by simply shrugging the latter angrily. Then she replied:—

"Eyes are made to look, and when one looks one sees; yet eyes have not the tongue to tell what they see, Masago." Turning her back upon the servant, the girl walked away.

The woman glided soundlessly across the room and disappeared into the narrow hall outside. Silent as was her going, yet Masago knew she was gone. She turned about with a sudden movement of passionate feeling.

"The woman knows!" she said, and clasped her hands spasmodically.

Then up and down she paced with unquiet feet, to stand still a moment, beating her hands softly together and biting the nails, and then again to pace the room. She threw herself upon the floor. Once again she drew the picture from her sleeve, to press it to her lips. After a while she sat up stiffly, as though she listened.

"Some one is without my shoji!" she said, rising uncertainly.

She heard dim voices whispering in the corridor; then suddenly the loud, shrill cry of a runner outside the house and the sing-song, mellow answer of the guide Oka.

"Heu! Heu! This way! Ah-ho! So!"

Her parents had returned home she thought, as she ran to the balcony. She leaned over the railing, forgetting the murmured voices she had already heard within the house itself.

"Mother! Father! You have returned!"

The cry of the runner floated up to her through the dark mist. Then the loud, hoarse cry of Oka, the guide, proclaiming:—

"August guests for the maid Masago-san."

The girl's eyes expressed astonishment.

Guests for her! and at such an hour! Surely that stupid maid would not admit them till she had learned their names and mission. She, Masago, was but a maiden and little used to receiving guests unchaperoned within her father's house. Masago had forgotten her vague thoughts of but a moment since. Now she was the simple daughter of a respectable household, agitated at the unexpected advent of evening guests.

"No doubt," she thought, "they come to see my father, who is not at home. I must descend and beseech them to remain and venture not out again into the fog, though Shaka knows I little wished for guests to-night."

Sighing, she turned back to her room. Within the light was soft but clear, for an officious one had brought in other andons, and by the hall sliding doors, which were opened, Masago saw a bright Takahiri (lantern) flickering without. By this light she saw a kneeling form, crouching with head to mats. Over her the servant who had brought Masago her evening meal stretched a hand to close the shoji.

Then Masago's eyes turned to that other one within her chamber, and coming to her face, were fixed. She started back a pace, her lips apart. Her visitor did not move or speak. In silent, strange absorption her eyes were fixed upon Masago's face. Thus for a long moment these two stood and looked upon each other, neither speaking, neither moving.

XIII

DAUGHTERS OF NIJO

Masago spoke, her words strangely enunciated.

"Lady—you—you desired to speak with me?"

Her voice broke the spell of silence. The visitor bowed her head simply but eloquently. Masago went a nervous step toward her. There was fear in both her face and voice as she began deprecatingly:—

"It was an honorable mistake, lady, that you were not shown within the ozashishi (guest room). I beg you, lady, will you not speak?"

Her fears overcame her politeness. There was something unreal, strange, almost spiritual, in this woman who looked at her with her own eyes. For Masago almost thought she dreamed, and that she stood before a magic mirror wherein she saw reflected her own beauteous image, clad as only in dreams. But the vision spoke, and Masago's fright vanished.

"It was my wish," she said in a low voice, "to see you in your chamber. I begged this privilege, Masago."

"Then, pray you, please be seated," urged the girl. She brought a mat and set it for the guest.

The visitor stooped, but not to the mat. She lifted up an andon, and carrying it in her hand went closer to Masago.

"A moment and I will be seated, but first I wish to see your face—quite close."

She held the light near to the countenance of Masago and scanned her startled features. Then, swinging it before her own, she said:

"Look you at mine also."

Masago started, with a thrill of wondering amaze.

"Now," said the other, "I will be seated, and pray you also, sit by me, Masago."

"I do not know you, lady," said Masago, with sudden brusqueness. "I pray you, speak your mission in my father's house."

The other smiled.

"Your father's house!" she repeated.

"Why do you repeat my words?" said Masago.

"I was told the Prince of Nijo—"

Masago started toward her with a little cry, and that same savage movement with which she had sprung upon the servant. Though inwardly she cherished thought of Nijo, she could not bear that others should speak of it.

"You come here to insult me!" she cried, her bosom heaving with suppressed excitement.

"Be not angry," said the other, softly. "I came but to speak the truth, and—and to gaze upon—my sister!"

"Sister!" The word escaped the lips of Masago like a cry of pain. "You—you are—"

"Sado-ko," she answered, smiling still, yet sadly.

A moment Masago stared at her dumbly, then with an indescribable movement she knelt down at the princess's feet and put her head upon the mats. Sado-ko bent over her, stooped, touching her head.

"I pray you, kneel not thus to me," she said.

Slowly Masago arose, the color flowing back into her pale face in a flood. Her eyes were bright and wide and feverish. That moment's servile impulse, when she had fallen down upon her knees, was past. She looked the Princess Sado-ko in the eyes, with conscious equality.

"Now," said the princess, simply, "will you not be seated?"

Silently the two sought the mats. Opposite each other they sat, each with her eyes upon the other. Each spoke at once, and each the same words:—

"You know then—"

"You know then—"

They bowed their heads. Thus both confessed their knowledge of the fact that not one of them, but both, were daughters of the Prince of Nijo, and hence sisters. Then Masago:—

"Why do you come to me, exalted princess? I am but a lowly maiden, who cannot even touch the hem of your kimono."

"There is a bitter tone within your voice," said Sado-ko. "Why is it so?"

Masago did not answer, and the princess continued:—

"Of your history I had learned, Masago. It matters not how or where or when. One spoke of you with—love—"

She broke off sharply to wring her hands unconsciously.

"And so I came to—to look upon you—sister."

"You came from curiosity," said Masago, in that same bitter tone. "It was the passing whim of a languid princess, bored with her greatness."

"You misjudge me," said the Princess Sado-ko, with a sigh.

ONOTO WATANNA

"Not so," replied Masago, the color flaming in her face; "I can but recognize that same idle fancy that also once possessed your father when he—"

She bit her lips and turned her face away. Angry tears clouded her eyes. She could not speak for her proud emotion.

"There was another reason," said the princess, softly. "Masago, pray turn not your head in pride from me. I came not out of condescension, nor yet from idle curiosity, but because of a strange hunger of my heart, which I could not resist."

"How can *you* have heart-hunger?" asked Masago, coldly.

"And why not I?" Her very voice was thrilling with its sadness. Masago would not look upon her face. She was conscious only of that raging jealousy and pain swelling up in her breast.

"And why not I?" repeated Sado-ko.

"You, who are a princess of the royal family!" cried Masago, with a sudden fierceness. "You, of whom all the poets in the realm have sung and raved! You, at whose feet the whole bright, glittering world is strewn! You, the cherished Daughter of the Sun—the bride-to-be of the—the Prince Komatzu!"

"But still a sad and wretched woman," said the Princess Sado-ko.

Masago turned upon her fiercely.

"And if you are so sad, as you say," she cried, "who can have pity for your sorrow? Are you, then, a statue that you do not appreciate these priceless gifts of all the gods?"

"Masago, gifts unsought are oftentimes not desired, and sometimes those which glitter in the sun do but reflect its light. What are the gilded outward wrappings of the gods to me, if inwardly still my heart breaks?"

"Your heart breaks!" Masago laughed in scorn. "What, you—who are about to marry the noblest, bravest, the most divine—" She broke off, holding her hands to her throat.

With a sudden movement the Princess Sado-ko bent forward and looked into the averted face of the maid Masago.

"You!" she cried, "you love this—" She could not finish her words.

Masago dropped her face within her hands.

"I," she said. "Yes, I—so humble—the daughter of—"

"The Prince of Nijo!" whispered Sado-ko.

Slowly the hands fell from the girl's face. Her eyes met those of Sado-ko's.

XIV

Solution of the Gods

A wild flush of color rushed to the face of Sado-ko; a light so clear as at first to dazzle her, flashed through her mind.

"Masago—sister!" she cried. "Oh, the gods give me solution of both our griefs!"

"There is, alas! none for mine," said Masago, and sullenly wiped away the tears.

"Listen!"

The Princess Sado-ko leaned over and spoke in a lowered voice.

"You are affianced to the artist, Kamura Junzo. Is it not so, Masago?"

A motion of impatient assent was the girl's reply.

"And you do not joyfully anticipate the union?"

"I loathe the very thought," returned Masago, bitterly.

The princess paused a moment as though to master her amazement.

"Loathe thought of union with Junzo!" she repeated, then laughed with almost childish joy. "It is not strange—in you, perhaps. Now listen once again, and pray you, answer me."

"I am listening," said Masago, with sullen impatience. "I will also answer, princess."

"Call me sister. Name me Sado-ko, I beg."

"I will call you princess."

"Perhaps you will not do so, Masago, when I have completed. But hear me. You love your home, of course, and also your good parents?"

"It is said I am of an honorably dutiful and filial temperament," replied Masago, coldly.

"But," continued Sado-ko, "there are other things you love still more than your dear home? It is possible?"

"It is so," replied Masago, briefly. "Do not look surprised, O princess. Homes are not all palaces, nor yet are parents all royal."

"Masago," said the princess gently, "a palace never makes a home, nor royalty a parent. Your home," she looked about her with approving eyes,—"it is most sweet and choice, Masago."

"The simple cottage of a merchant," said Masago.

"Your parents—they are kind?"

"They are kind," said Masago, and for the first time flushed with some evident feeling.

"And you have little brothers—yes?" Sado-ko's voice was wistful.

"Five brothers. They are noisy, and sometimes, princess, rough and most uncouth, and therefore tiresome."

"But loving. You will grant that?"

"Oh, yes!"

"You were unhappy—you missed them, did you not, when you left them for the school, Masago?"

"I was free," said the girl, slowly.

"Free! Free from loving home, from parents—Junzo—all who loved you. Free! You prize such freedom, Masago?"

The girl remained silent, her head drooping, her brows drawn. Suddenly she raised her face defiantly.

"I am not unappreciative of their good qualities. It was not my fault that I was fashioned—so!" She smote her hands against her breast with an eloquent gesture.

"Yet, I confess, since I was but a little child, I have felt like one oppressed—caged—stifled! Still I was deemed submissive! My lips were sealed in silence. I was patient, for only once did I protest against the dull monotony of my lot. I asked Yamada Kwacho for just one year of freedom. I did not name it such, but such it was. For this small respite, Sado-ko, I tied my life to another's and affianced myself to Junzo. It was a bitter moment."

"You did not love him?" asked the princess, in a timid, most beseeching voice.

"I did not even look upon him," returned Masago, impatiently. "He was my father's choice, not mine. I—see, look here, O princess!" She held before the eyes of Sado-ko the printed picture of the Prince Komatzu, then continued swiftly, with passionate vehemence:—

"This was my hero! I went up to Kyoto not to study."

She arose and began to walk across the chamber, clasping and unclasping her hands as she spoke.

"I saw the noble palaces of my ancestors,—yes, mine! I lingered, wandered in the streets outside—think of it!—outside the walls! I watched at every gate, and saw the cortèges and the trains of the nobles and the princes pass and repass back and forth; and oh! while I must fall upon my face—I! And once, just once, I touched the august sword of Prince Komatzu. Thus! It was thus I did so."

She swung her long sleeve till it barely grazed the head of Sado-ko, in illustration.

"'Twas in a public place he spoke. They set him up like any common man! He was so noble, so great. O princess! he spoke to all that gaping herd like man to man, with less of condescension than the lordly politicians of the capital,—he whose august feet should not have deigned to touch the earth."

"Nay," interposed the princess, smiling quietly, "Komatzu is a modern. The times have changed, Masago. No longer are the royal ones called gods."

"Yet like unto a god he was," declared the girl, "for I saw with these eyes."

"Which love had sweetly blinded," smiled the princess, sympathetically. She, also, arose, and put her hand upon Masago's arm, leaning against her.

"Masago," she said, in her low, winning voice, "if you could do so, would you change your simple home for the royal court and all its glamour?"

"Ask the birds if they prefer the wide, free sky to the dark sea."

"Would you, then, exchange your state for—mine, Masago?"

Slowly the girl turned her face and looked into the pleading eyes of Sado-ko. Her voice was hoarse. She said:—

"You give me wilful pain, O princess. Why? You know full well that could not be."

"Why not?" asked Sado-ko, whisperingly.

"No, no!" Masago recoiled, her incredulous eyes fixed as if fascinated on the face of Sado-ko. The princess placed her hands on the shoulders of Masago, and brought her face close to hers.

"Look into the mirror—Sado-ko," said she.

"Sado-ko! You call me by your name!"

"And pray you, call me—Masago."

"Oh, no! Oh, no!"

"You will not change with me?"

"Oh, oh!" Masago had become white as death, as though she were about to faint.

"Will you not do so?" still pleaded the now almost despairing voice of Sado-ko.

"I dare not—dare not," she murmured.

There was silence now in the room. The dim sounds of the world about them did not reach the ears of these two. Masago had reached out a trembling hand to support herself against the framework of the wall. Sado-ko watched her with a yearning, melancholy expression in her face. Suddenly she turned away.

"You were right, Masago," she said slowly. "It could not be." She paused, then, sighing, moved with drooping head toward the doors of the corridor.

"Sayonara—sister," she softly breathed.

That word of farewell broke the tension of the dazed Masago. She sprang with a cry after the departing one. Both of the princess's sleeves were in her grasp.

"Go not yet!" she cried. "Do not go!"

She fell grovelling upon her knees, still clinging to the long sleeves of the princess, and hid her face in the folds of Sado-ko's kimono. Then, with her face muffled in the gown, she spoke:—

"I could not grasp the meaning of your words—My heart leaped up and burst—I could not think. I pray you, do not take my joy away while yet I barely grasp it in my hands, Princess Sado-ko!"

"You do consent!" said Sado-ko, bending over her, while a strange light of excitement came into her eyes.

"Consent! On my knees I could pray to you, as to a god, to grant this thing you suggest for a caprice."

XV

The Change

"Hush! Do not speak so loudly, Masago!"

"How you tremble, Sado-ko."

"We have once more mistaken our names," said she who was the Princess Sado-ko.

"Oh, true. Now call me Sado-ko! No, call me noble princess, most divine, exalted, august, royal princess! Call me so!"

"A princess is not so addressed," replied the other, smiling, "save sometimes by a servile, ignorant one."

"I fear I will be sure to make the most absurd mistakes."

"So! Then the whole court will call it 'A new caprice of the foolish Princess Sado-ko.'"

"Again, if you please—call me Sado-ko."

"Princess Sado-ko!"

"Masago!"

"Nay, call me simply 'sister,'" said the other, in a trembling voice.

"Sister—there! Does not this beauteous robe become me well?"

"As though it were made alone for you, Masago."

"No, no,—Princess Sado-ko!"

"I bow my humble head unto the dust, most royal Princess Sado-ko!"

In mock humility the new Masago bowed before the old Masago.

"Yet," said the latter, with her red lips pursed in thought, "they say it is the latest fashion of the court to wear the foreign style of dress. Is it not so?"

"Yes. It is so."

"Oh, joyful! Such beautiful and gorgeous gowns as I shall wear. I will send at once to all the most famous foreign cities. Let me see,—to Holland, and to—"

"The Princess Sado-ko never liked the foreign gown," interrupted the other, shaking her head a trifle sadly.

"But you spoke just now of the caprices of that same Princess Sado-ko. She has already another one."

Then up and down the room, in the long, trailing robe of Princess Sado-ko, walked, peacock-like, the maiden Masago; while close at hand, with dreamy face and dewy eyes, clad in a simple crêpe kimono, and with flowers—no longer jewels—in her hair, stood Sado-ko.

"Tell me," said the vain and eager Masago, "when the noble Prince Komatzu shall greet me so,"—she bowed with assumed gallantry—"will I bow thus?" Down to the mat she bent her head.

"Why, no; but thus." Gracefully, simply she illustrated. "A low, but not too low, obeisance. You are of equal rank, Masa—princess!"

"So—like this?"

"No; this way."

"Well, it will take me twenty hours to practise thus. I will not sleep till I accomplish it."

"Oh, you will learn. Bow as you will, Masago. Komatzu will declare your mood has changed, and still insist that you are fair."

Stooping in her posing, Masago stared a moment at the other.

"Perhaps already he has whispered words of love to you, then?" Her voice was sharply jealous.

"No, my cousin does not know me quite as yet. You will make him better acquainted with Princess Sado-ko."

"Ah, that I will!"

She raised her long, slim arms from out the graceful sleeves. Her hands she clasped behind her head.

"Oh, what a glorious dream it is!" she said; then, in quick alarm, "A dream? Say that it is not all a dream."

But Sado-ko sat staring quietly into the future. When she raised her eyes, they softly gleamed.

"A dream it is—a dream, and yet—Oh, Kuonnon, let us not awake!"

"Ah, how can you be so glad—you who are to stay here only Masago?"

"Masago," repeated the other, softly. "That is well." She raised a flushing face. "I am like a bird set free, Masago. My very voice is sore to sing."

Masago threw herself upon the floor beside her.

"That is how I feel, also," she said.

They smiled into each other's faces, then drew closer together, their sympathy for each other growing.

"Here is some homely counsel," said Masago. "Confide small matters to my mother, and lead her on to gossip much with you. She will tell you everything there is to know. She is so simple—so foolish. A little wit upon your part will quickly disarm any suspicion she might have. But be not free in speech with Yamada Kwacho, your new father. A cold and constrained space has always been between us. Do not let the children disturb you with their prattle, and oh, also, pray you show some pride to certain neighbors, for none in all the town have had the same upbringing as Masago."

"And is that all,—these simple facts that I must heed to be Masago?"

"All. It is a dull and simple life."

"And you. Pray trust not the ladies of my suite. They do most heartily detest the Princess Sado-ko, who is given to seclusion, which has often deprived them of much gay pleasures of the new court."

"But I will change all that," said Masago.

"That is true." She sighed. "Well, then, there is nothing else to say. But stay! My maiden, Natsu-no. Oh, pray you, dear Masago, treat her with the greatest kindness, will you not?"

"I will."

"She is even now without this room, waiting for me, with that dear patience with which she watches and guards me at all times. You know, Masago, she has been with me since I was but a baby. Alas, I shall suffer for her loss!"

Tears for a moment dimmed the eyes of Sado-ko.

"What more?" asked Masago, surveying with delight the width and beauty of her obi.

"What else? Well, Masago, there is one other matter. In the garden of the Palace Nijo there hangs an open cage, just without my chamber. It is the home of my dear nightingale."

"A bird?"

"A little bird. Listen, there is a pretty story you would like to hear. Once in the spring, while I was yet a little girl, and grieving for my most beloved grandmother, his Majesty, the Emperor, sent me as a gift of consolation a nightingale within a golden cage. It sang so sweetly to me that I was entranced with delight, and when the days were warm would hang the cage upon my balcony. The garden close at hand was fragrant with the odor of the cherry and the plum, and allured many other nightingales to make their home there. The little birds noticed their play-mate in the cage, and when, at evening, they saw no one in sight—for I was hidden behind my shoji screen—they would approach the cage, and sing all merrily together. These honorably sweet serenades gave me double joy, as you may imagine, and I soon learned to distinguish the voices without and that one within the cage. At first I thought the song of my own bird within the cage sounded sweeter even than those without. Then in a little while it became hard to distinguish them, and at last I could not hear the voice of my small nightingale at all."

She paused a moment, as though in thought, then resumed, her eyes sweet with moisture.

"I pondered over this odd change, Masago, and then I thought that it must be because those without enjoyed their freedom in the open air, while my poor little bird was shut within the narrow limits of its cage."

Her eyes became more tender still as she proceeded.

"So I opened wide the door, Masago, and let my little bird go free."

"Why, then," spoke the other, "it is gone. How foolish you were, Sado-ko."

The princess shook her head.

"I thought, like you, that it would fly far, far away, but no! It only flew above my head a space, then soft alighted on a cherry tree close by, and filled the air with its sweet song."

"But since?"

"Since then, Masago, the cage is always opened wide. Yet still the nightingale makes its home within."

"It is a pretty tale," said Masago, thoughtfully, "but I should fear to lose the bird."

She arose and began once more to survey the long folds of her silken gown.

Sado-ko looked at her in silence, an expression of wistfulness about her eyes.

"It must be late," said Masago. "The fog is thick without. Should I not go now?"

Silently the princess arose.

"You are eager to try the new life," she said, smiling sadly, then sighing.

"Yes, I am eager," said Masago. "Who would not be?"

"Oka, the guide, is without, Masago. He is safe, is he not?"

"Oh, surely."

"Then there will be no peril in your return to Aoyama?"

"Oh, none," said Masago, then hesitated a moment. "But I do not think I will go there to-night." She appeared to be turning something over in her mind. The princess watched her doubtful face.

"I would much rather go to Tokyo straightway," said Masago.

"That is well, then," the other assented. "But first you will need to go up to the palace, for there your attendants still remain. Then I would advise that you leave to-night by norimono. Speak little to the maiden,

Natsu-no, who is keen-eared and keener eyed; but if you so desire, make inquiries of the Madame Bara, the chaperone. She is absent-minded and stupid."

"I do not wish to travel by norimon," said Masago. Then clasping her hands, she said, "Oh, I have long desired to travel in great royal state in a private train, such as it is said the Prince Komatzu uses."

"Very well, then. But give your orders at the palace. You will be obeyed. And now—you are going?"

"Shaka! I begin to tremble."

"And I," said Sado-ko, tremulously.

"Will not the maid discover—"

"Masago, bear in mind, the maid is but a maid. Treat her so."

"Ah, true! Yet you bade me be most kind to her."

"Kind, but not familiar."

"Oh, I will try. Now, what must I do to call her?"

"Why, clap your hands."

"So simple a signal for a princess?"

"Yes. Just so. I will illustrate."

Her little signal sounded sharp and clear. Masago started and trembled at its sound. Then she turned toward the opening doors. She heard the low voice of the princess whispering close beside her.

"Speak to her. Say, 'Maid, take up the light.'"

Masago walked with faltering steps toward the doors. Her voice shook a moment, then raised in nervousness, it sounded oddly harsh.

"Take up the light!" she said.

But at her voice the sleepy Natsu-no started, turned, and looked up at her face in wide-eyed surprise and growing fear; then her eyes went slowly to that other one, now with her back toward her near the shadow of the shoji, the bright outline of her huge obi bow alone in the light. Natsu-no, shaking and trembling, advanced a pace toward her, glancing fearfully meanwhile at that object standing there in her mistress's habiliments, yet in so strange and unfamiliar aspect.

Masago moved to cover her intense nervousness. The maid's voice quavered.

"Exalted princess, I—I—" She stammered over her words. Self-confidence asserted itself in Masago. She raised her head imperiously.

"Take up the light and follow me!" she said.

Trembling, dumb, and horror-stricken, the maid obeyed, for she had caught one quick, clear glimpse of that sweet other face.

XVI

A FAMILY COUNCIL

The Kamura house was built on a hill slope. Of all the houses of the suburb, it was nearest to the palace Aoyama. Shortly after the Restoration the elder Kamura had been a retainer of a kuge in the service of his late Majesty. Thus he received permission to build his house near to the summer chariot (throne) of the Sons of Heaven (Imperial family).

It was a restful dwelling, its lower story surrounded by verandas, while small, flower-laden balconies were upon the upper story. The gardens were artistic in their arrangement, showing the youthful labors of Junzo and his younger brothers. In his earlier years Junzo had been ambitious to become an artist gardener,—a most honorable calling in Japan,—and so upon the few acres of land belonging to his father he had spent the first passion of the artist.

With the aid of his brothers he had carried from the river heaps of white pebbles, which were placed at angles of the flower beds; while between the pebbles the fine embroidered ferns pushed up their fresh green heads. A trellis-work arched the garden gate, weighted down by vines and wistaria. The arms of the pine were trimmed; a stately camphor tree shaded the house verandas. At intervals through the garden, cherry, plum, peach, and quince trees contributed their share of blossoms, fruit, and fragrance.

From the upper story the outlook was picturesque. To the eastward were the Aoyama parks and the white walls of the palace gardens; on the north, beyond the wooded parks, were mountain ranges; on the west the village, Kamakura, close to the shore of the playful yet mist-dangerous Hayama; while to the southward, over the hills and through the valleys, the great white highway led to Tokyo.

On the afternoon of the family council the guests were ushered upstairs, where all the shojis had been removed, thus making a cool pavilion of the story. Every male relative of the Kamura family had dutifully accepted the invitation, since they were old-fashioned and most punctilious in the observance of family and social etiquette.

After the usual exchange of salutations, Madame Kamura and her young daughter, Haru-no, brought tea and tobacco for the men.

Then with graceful prostrations they made their excuses, and, taking Ohano with them, retired to another portion of the house. The women's retirement was the signal for the council's beginning.

Kamura, the first to speak, showed apparent reluctance, while at the same time he nervously tapped his pipe upon the hibachi.

"Honorable relatives," he said, bowing to the company, and then turning toward Yamada Kwacho, "and most esteemed friend and neighbor, it gives me pain to be forced to make apology for the absence of my son Junzo."

He paused, and, to cover his discomposure, solemnly filled and lighted his pipe again, while the relatives masked their surprise with polite, impassive expressions.

"My son," continued Kamura, "arrived last night from Tokyo. I doubt not for a moment, but that it was his honorable purpose and intention to attend our council, which you all know was called to arrange the preliminaries of the wedding ceremony of my son, Kamura Junzo, and the most virtuous and estimable Masago."

Again the old man paused to glance in a half-appealing way at his son Okido, the next in age to Junzo, who sat at his left side. On Kamura's right the seat was vacant. This was Junzo's place.

"Last night," continued Kamura, "my son was certainly ill in health; he was pale of face and absent in both look and speech. I set it down to the most natural mood of youth about to wed. We all, good sirs, have felt that happy sense of melancholy peculiar to this stage of our careers."

Some of the guests smiled, and nodded their heads, assenting to this fact; others looked at one another somewhat dubiously.

"And so," continued their host, "we thought it wisdom not to broach the subject of our council. When morning came Junzo was still pale and constrained. His mother spoke in delicate terms of the council planned, and he mildly acquiesced in all she said. At noon he barely touched his meal. He appeared so listless, that no member of the family had the heart to break upon his meditations. Hence, when he walked in seeming moodiness about the gardens, then suddenly turned and wandered toward the hills, I simply bade my son Okido follow him at respectful distance. To be more brief, good friends, it seems that Junzo followed a straight course along the hills, and, coming to the palace walls of Aoyama, ventured beyond the gates. Okido, being an obedient and filial son, hastened home to acquaint his father with the facts. Since then my son has not returned."

"He ventured beyond the palace gates!" exclaimed Yamada Kwacho. "Had he a pass, Kamura?"

"I do not know," said the old man, simply. "You have already heard my son has fame at court. I have accounted for his absent state of mind by the fact that, being young and new to favor, his mind is filled with thought of his art and work."

"And he has not returned?" queried sharply an uncle.

"Not yet," said Kamura, bowing courteously.

"I trust he has not come to harm," said another relative, with concern. "It is said the palace once again is opened, and that the noble Princess Sado-ko is there in maiden retirement."

"There is time for his return," declared Kamura, with dignity. "I trust you all will stay with me. What say you, my good friend Kwacho?"

"Assuredly, I will stay," assented the gruff and honest Kwacho.

"And I."

"And I."

Thus from all the guests.

They sat late into the afternoon, beguiled by saké, tea, and the dreamy day. The mellow light of the sun was softly dulled by the white haze which crept up to the sky from out the river. The white mist deepened, turning softly gray, then darkened imperceptibly. A breeze sprang up from the west, sweeping with briskness through the opened story of the Kamura house.

Yamada Kwacho contracted his brows, as he looked uneasily at the darkened sky. As though he read his thoughts, the patient voice of his host said simply:—

"It is but the hour of four."

"Yet see how strangely, weirdly dark," said a young cousin, pointing out toward the river. "There seems a cloud upon the Hayama, Cousin Kamura."

"A habit of this country hereabouts," said Kwacho, answering for his host. "Sometimes the mists arise while it is yet noon, and, creeping across the skies, darken and thicken in a fog so dense that even a tailless cat might lose its way."

The young Kamura cousin shuddered, and looked with apprehension at the ever clouding sky.

Yet time slipped quickly by for these easeful, somewhat indolent Japanese, who lounged, smoked, and sipped their saké, unmindful of the mist.

"The fog is spreading," said the youth Okido. "Shall we not close the shoji walls and bring andons for our honored guests?"

"My son has not returned," said the gentle voice of the father; "yet—" He glanced about uneasily, in the deepening shadow, scarcely able to distinguish one guest from another. He arose, and shook the skirt of his hakama. In a moment he recalled that, father though he was, yet he was still a host. He clapped his hands, and bade the answering servant close the shoji walls, and bring lights.

It was not five o'clock in the afternoon, yet the gray world without told of close creeping night.

At six the ladies of the house came to the upper story. Madame Kamura was pale; her daughter, a young girl of seventeen, showed a somewhat frightened countenance, while Ohano alone was placid, and seemingly contented of mind.

The fog grew thicker every moment, Madame Kamura told her husband, and as she feared it was not possible their guests could leave the house that night, she had ordered dinner served, and would prepare the sleeping chambers. She spoke only of the comfort of her guests. Although Junzo had not returned, no words escaped her careful lips of that which wrenched her mother-heart.

Her husband thanked her for her thoughtfulness, and said that they would be ready for the honorable meal, but begged her not to speak of rest. They would keep the council until the midnight hour.

And so the evening meal was served. The night was spent in quiet saké sipping, and dreamy introspection by the guests, while the heart of the genial host was heavy.

In a chamber of the lower story Ohano snored in healthy forgetfulness of all the little ills of life. The maiden Haru-no drowsed by the shoji of the Ozashiki; and by her side, immovable and silent, but with wide, wakeful eyes, the mother of Kamura Junzo kept the night watch.

"It is the fate of the humble female," she had protested, when the young Haru-no had begged her to sleep. "Bear this precept, daughter, always in your mind: The mother, wife, the sister, daughter, must ever watch and wait upon the comfort of the male. It is the law; it is our duty; it is our fate. We bow to it with submissive philosophy."

At twelve there was a stir upon the upper floor. Madame Kamura heard the shuffling movement of the breaking of the council. By the drowsy footfalls she knew the guests were anxious for their beds. She bade a servant attend the guests. Then she returned to her station. She did not turn her head when the sound of footsteps passed along the hall. Her husband quietly took his place by her side, without speaking. Thus all night long these two kept watch for Junzo.

XVII

The New Masago

The following morning dawned clear and bright, not a remnant of mist or fog remaining to recall the previous night. A bright yellow sun arose from behind the hills and beat away every vista of gloom from the skies. It poised above the river Hayama, as though to look upon its own reflected light; then swept along its early course, flooding the land with new light, and piercing the shoji walls of the chamber of the maid Masago.

The Princess Sado-ko opened her eyes, looked half dazedly, half wonderingly, a moment at the unfamiliar ceiling overhead, then sat up on the mattress. Her eyes wandered about the room in a helpless, bewildered fashion for a moment, then suddenly a little flickering smile of recollection came. She slipped from the mosquito netting.

She was in pale blue linen. Below her gown her little bare feet twinkled over the matting as she hastily crossed the room, pushed the casement a small way open, and peeped without. A breath of delight escaped her, for from Masago's chamber her eyes looked out upon the old delightful scenes of her childhood, the far-reaching meadows, sloping hills, and Fuji-Yama smiling in the morning light.

For some time she remained by the casement, enjoying simply the morning and its gentle breezes. Almost unconsciously she found herself waiting for the attendance of her maiden, Natsu-no. Then recalling Masago's words that henceforth she must robe herself, she laughed.

She had no difficulty in dressing. Masago's wardrobe was of the simplest, Yamada Kwacho limiting her in dress expenditure. Sado-ko donned a pretty plum-colored crêpe kimono and a dark, gold-figured obi. Her hands fluttered delightedly over Masago's clothes; they were so simple and comfortable, she thought.

When she was quite dressed, she forgot to put away the bed,—a duty Masago always performed,—but stepping out upon the balcony loitered for a moment in the sun. Then the garden's fragrance captivating her, she ran down the little flight of stairs into the garden.

Flowers grew abundantly there,—simple and common flowers they were, but preferred by Kwacho because of their very lack of cultivation, and hence their naturalness.

Almost recklessly Sado-ko plucked them, filling her arms with blossoms. She had an inclination to sing and laugh and pick flowers all the day, she felt so strangely free and happy.

When a servant came and watched her from the kitchen door, the girl smiled toward her. The woman appeared taken aback at the good will in the girl's face. Masago had been over-bearing toward her father's servants, which had made her generally unpopular among them. The servant's voice was not so sharp as she had intended it to be. Would Masago have her morning meal?

The young girl in the sunny garden nodded cheerfully, then hastened toward the house, her flowers in her arms. She drank her morning tea in happy silence, but smiled so often at the waiting maid, that the latter marvelled at her amiability of mood. When Sado-ko had finished, the woman said, almost in a deprecating tone:—

"I did not mean to give offence last night, Masago."

"Offence?" repeated Sado-ko. "Did you give offence—to me?"

"Why, yes. Do you not recall my looking at the picture in your hands?"

"What picture? Oh, yes, yes. Did you do so? Now I do recall it."

She moved toward the door to cover her confusion, then turned her head backward, smiling sweetly at the servant.

"Do not worry, maid. I am not offended."

A moment the woman stared at her in bewilderment. Then she said with some hesitancy:

"Before you went to Kyoto, Masago, I always took the liberties with you, which since your late return you appeared not to desire. I, being long in your family service, as you know, was hurt."

Sado-ko paused in the doorway.

"When—when did I return?" she asked, in a curious tone, as though she could not recall the exact date. "I have been away it seems—yes—I have been away; but when did I return?"

"Why, only two days since," declared the maid, in astonishment.

"How absent is my little mind," she laughed. "Two days ago. Why, yes, of course—and let me see, I have been gone—" She appeared to calculate the time.

"But half a year," said the servant. "You were to have stayed one year, but your affianced, having acquired such great fame at court, your father wished to hasten on your honorable marriage."

"Oh," said the girl, and then repeated in a low, happy voice, "hasten on my marriage."

She turned suddenly toward the maid.

"Do you find me changed?" she asked.

The woman regarded her dubiously.

"Ye-es—no. Last night I thought you more than usually impatient, Masago."

"Ah—was I so? I did not mean it."

"But to-day you seem more kind than even as a child, though you were the most gentle, passive, and best of little ones."

"And so I am just now," said Sado-ko, merrily. "I am not changed one little bit. Think of me, if you please, as a child."

"Perhaps the fault was mine last night," pursued the woman, glad to prolong the conversation with Masago.

"Look!" exclaimed the girl, pointing to the garden. "See, some little children!"

"Your brothers, Masago. Can you not see?"

"Brothers—mine! Oh-h!"

Dropping her flowers on the veranda, she ran lightly down the path, as though to meet the little boys. Halfway down the path a sense of panic seized upon the princess. She paused in painful hesitancy, scarce knowing which way to turn.

Would not these little brothers of Masago recognize the deception? Could the likeness be so strong as to deceive Masago's own family? A maid's judgment was but a poor criterion.

She stood quite still, waiting, yet dreading their approach. Her first impulse had been to run in loving fashion to meet the little boys. Her sudden fear of these individuals saved her from doing that which Masago never had done, caress or fondle her small brothers.

While Sado-ko possessed an innate love of nature and of children, these things but irritated poor Masago, who called the country dull, the town enchanting, children wearisome, and fashion fascinating. Though each feature of the faces of these two sisters was identically alike, their natures vastly differed. Sado-ko was all her mother in nature, and even the cold harshness of her life had frozen but her exterior self. Masago was the complement of Prince Nijo. Her previous environment, association with Ohano, and possibly a little portion of the latter's nature made her what she was,—a girl of weak and vain ambitions.

Now the princess stood hesitating, fearfully, before the little army of Masago's brothers, five in all. The older ones spoke her name respectfully, as they had been taught to do. The smaller ones pulled her sleeves and obi mischievously, as though they sought to tease her; but when she laughed, they seemed abashed, and ran to hide behind a tree from whence they peered at her.

The maid who brought them from the neighbor's bade the girl an apathetic good morning, and seemed surprised at the cordiality of the other's greeting.

Sado-ko breathed with some relief as the children disappeared within the house. Then for the first time she sighed wistfully.

"If they had loved Masago," she said, "surely they would miss her. But no, a stranger steps into her clothes, takes her place within the house, and fickle childhood cannot see."

In gentle depression she moved toward the house, then slowly up the steps to Masago's balcony, from which she watched the children take their morning bath in the family pond. It was a pretty sight, she thought, to see their little bare, brown bodies shining in the sun. A little later the elder children went whistling down the path to school while the nurse disappeared with the younger ones.

"Strange," said Princess Sado-ko, "that none of them seemed glad to see their sister. Was not Masago loved, then?"

She pushed the doors open and thoughtfully entered the chamber.

"Perhaps," she said, "the foreigners speak truth. What is that pretty proverb of their honorable religion? Is it not, 'The love begets the love'? Masago plainly did not love her little brothers. Hence they have but indifference for her."

Again she sighed.

"Ah," she said, "what kind of maiden, then, is this I have exchanged for me?"

She saw the tumbled couch upon which she had slept. She recalled the fact that Masago had told her she would be required to make her own bed and attend her own chamber, for Kwacho deemed such household tasks desirable and admirable in a woman.

Therefore the exalted Princess Sado-ko, the daughter of the sun-god, as she was called by all loyal Japanese, fell to work upon the homely employment of rolling up a mattress bed, beating the little rocking pillow, folding the quilts and the netting. Suddenly she sat down breathlessly among the simple paraphernalia which constituted Masago's bed. She had forgotten where the maid Masago had told her the clothes were kept! The little thought perplexed and troubled the Princess Sado-ko.

XVIII

A Mother Blind

While the Princess Sado-ko was sitting ruefully among the folded bed things, and pondering upon the weighty question of their disposal, Kwacho and Ohano arrived home in jinrikishas. The former hastened to the kitchen for a cup of tea before departing on a mission to Tokyo, while Ohano hurried up the stairs to her daughter. Ohano was so eager to pour out recent confidences to her daughter, that she labored at every step in her ascent.

When she entered Masago's room without knocking, as was her custom, she was astonished at the sudden start the girl gave. However, Ohano had such a story to pour out that she did not pause, but said in almost one breath:—

"Masago, I have the greatest news for you—it will make you the happiest of maidens in Kamakura—What! your bedclothes not put away yet? Well—but I must tell you all that happened, at once."

She broke off breathlessly, her eyes upon the young girl's face. Something unfamiliar and strange about it stopped her flying tongue. She stared at her in stupefied perplexity, her mouth wide open.

Sado-ko averted her face. With her head slightly turned, she stood in a listening attitude, as though waiting for Ohano to proceed.

"How strangely you looked at me just now!" gasped Ohano, and, leaning over, pulled her sleeve. "Masago! You have not spoken to me yet!"

"I have not had the chance," said Sado-ko, in a stifled voice.

"Why—your voice is strange! What has happened, daughter?"

Sado-ko attempted to recover her composure, fighting against a sense of weakness that overpowered her at the thought that Ohano would penetrate the disguise. What mother would not have done so? she thought with fear. With some bravado she turned and faced Ohano.

"Nothing is the matter," she declared. "You—you said you had some news to tell me, mother." She bit her lip at the last word, as the thought came to her that this woman might not be the mother. The words of Ohano reassured her.

"Well, come and sit here," she said. "I have much to tell."

When Sado-ko was seated at her side with averted face, the words of the mother became piteous.

"Your mother always was so stupid," said poor Ohano, "but, Masago, you really are much changed since your return from school. Yet truly—why, I never noticed it before." She stopped as though to give the girl a chance to speak, but the latter remained silent.

"Now let me see," said Ohano, "I will tell you from the first of all that happened. I know, Masago, you will be happy at my news. You see, we waited all the day and all the night for him to come and—"

"For *him*?" said Sado-ko, in a low voice.

"Yes—for Junzo."

"Junzo!" She turned toward Ohano with a sudden swiftness. Her eyes were dilated with trembling excitement, "Yes, yes—pray speak on."

Pausing, Ohano looked in astonishment at the girl's flushing face.

"Ah, now I know why you seem changed, Masago," she said finally. "It was thinking all night long upon your wedding. Well, who could blame a maiden for feeling and for acting somewhat—changed?"

"But tell me," said the girl, pleadingly, "of—of Junzo. Why do you not proceed?"

"Well, we waited for him all the day, Masago, and all the—"

"You have already said that. Do proceed."

"He did not come."

"Not come! Why, where—"

"You hardly give me breath to speak to-day, Masago. Do not hasten my words so. I told you that I had good news for you. Be patient, as a maiden should be, and hear my story."

"Yes, yes, yes."

"Well, your affianced did not come. Is not that welcome news for you?"

Sado-ko smote her hands together. She had become white, and her lips were quivering.

"Why did he not come?"

Ohano shrugged her plump shoulders.

"The gods alone know why, Masago. It seems he went out early in the day before the fog arose, and—Why, how you startle me to-day!"

With a half-stifled cry the princess sprang to her feet, and stood before Ohano trembling in agitation.

"You do not mean that he has met with harm?" she cried in a horrified tone. "Oh, you sit there smiling when my heart is bursting with its fear. Why do you not explain—"

Her breath came in gasps. She could scarcely enunciate her words. Ohano stared up at her aghast.

"Shaka, Masago! You are beside yourself with most incomprehensible agitation."

With an eloquent, piteous gesture the girl threw out her hands.

"Oh, will you not tell me what has happened to him?" she cried.

"Happened to whom? You do not mean to Junzo?"

Sado-ko nodded her head and clasped her hands.

"Who else could I mean?" she asked.

"Well, nothing that we know has happened to the man," said Ohano. "He simply would not come to his own marriage council. The reason is most plain, I think."

"But the fog—you spoke of it—" The girl was now upon the verge of tears.

"The fog was good excuse for his absence, Masago. Yet no one of the guests believed it was the reason he did not come; and when this morning brought a guard from Aoyama, why, even the most stupid of us all—your simple mother—knew the cause of your fiancé's absence, and why he went to Tokyo."

The girl repeated the words dazedly. "To Tokyo!"

"So the guard declared. He said that Junzo followed the norimon of the Princess Sado-ko down to the railway station—then—"

Ohano paused at the odd exclamation which escaped the girl.

"Sado-ko!" she said in a soft voice, then began to laugh in a strange fashion.

"Do not mind my silly laughter. I—I am not well to-day. Continue, if you please. Do not stop."

Ohano looked concerned, but continued obediently.

"The guard informed us that when they reached the station Junzo, acting like one crazed, sought passage on the royal train. This being denied him, he followed on the next, while his parents and relations, and good Kwacho and myself, were waiting for his coming at his father's house. There is only one solution."

The girl was laughing softly, yet in a strangely tearful way. She said:—

"He followed Sado-ko!"

"Just so, Masago. She is his patroness, and I have heard—But never mind, you look so pale this morning I will not gossip of that other

ONOTO WATANNA

matter. His parents say the honor paid him at the court has turned his head, but I am of another thought." She shook her head knowingly. "It is my firm belief, Masago, despite the smooth words of his family and the rough ones of your father, that Junzo went away because he dreaded thought of wedding you. He has another fancy."

Sado-ko smiled through her tears.

"It is true," she said, "I do not doubt it. He dreaded thought of union with Masago."

"Just as you, Masago," said Ohano, bridling, "dreaded the thought of marrying him. You were ill suited to each other. The gods know best."

"Yes," said the princess, softly, "the gods know best."

She looked out through the casement toward the hills of Aoyama. As though she spoke to herself, she said:—

"He will return. He will understand." Then, in a lower voice, "He loves me."

Ohano, engaged in putting away the bedding, had not heard the latter words. As she set them, neatly folded, in a little cupboard, she said in tones of conviction:—

"Do not worry, daughter. He will not return. The gods have given you the freedom that you wished so much. Be thankful—"

Sado-ko did not hear her words. She went to the balcony, and looked with wistful eyes toward her former castle home.

"He will return," she whispered to her questioning heart, "I am not stranded here alone."

A thrill of apprehension smote her. Had the change she had effected with Masago been in vain? Would Junzo follow the new Sado-ko? Could it be that his eyes were no keener than those of Masago's relatives?

All about her the yellow sunlight smiled. The hills were warm. The skies were blue. The air was still and sweet. Peace and silence were everywhere in Kamakura.

"The gods are good," said Sado-ko, with divine faith; "he must return to me."

XIX

WITHIN THE PALACE NIJO

The palace Nijo, the resort of West-desiring nobility and court, was possibly the oddest if most expensive residence in Tokyo. Originally it had been a Yashiki of the Daimio of Mito. Time and the impulsive treatment of the Imperialists had demolished portions of the place. With each persistent rebuilding, strangely enough, the palace took on a more modern, foreign aspect, until this time, when, in spite of its ancient moat, quite dry and overgrown with trees, its lodges, and its few melancholy turrets, it bore a strong resemblance to those houses built upon the bluffs of Yokohama by the foreign residents.

The Nijo palace in itself was a monument to the country's change. Bit by bit its ancient Eastern aspect was disappearing, so that now, except for the rambling character of portions of its yashiki-like walls, and its enormous size, it was as Western in outward looks as the Japanese modern himself appeared when clad in Western dress.

Even its grounds were typical of the new era, for close-clipped lawns replaced the gardens, groves, shrines, fish-ponds, hillocks, and artificial landscapes, once the rule within the walls of this yashiki.

No longer at the palace gates the lordly, haughty man of swords scowled upon the passer-by. The days of the samurai and ancient chivalry were dead,—since but a score of years. So rapid was the sweeping "progress" of the new Japan! Now stiff guards, in heavy foreign uniform, patrolled the grounds; while within the house itself the very servants wore the buttoned livery of the West. Fashion shook her foolish hand over the city of Tokyo, and her subjects, adoring and submissive as ever, named her guilelessly, "Progression."

Within the palace Nijo all wore the garb of Europe,—the thick, sticking, heavy cloth of man, and the tight, suffocating dress of woman. The gentleman of fashion and means, at this time, possessed two residences, a town and country place,—sometimes several of the latter.

In Tokyo foreign life and foreign dress ruled supreme at court, save, possibly, within the secret privacy of chambers, when heated men and panting women flung aside their Western garb, and, sighing breaths of eased relief, slipped on the soft and cool hakama or kimono.

Junzo, the artist of Kamakura, had no difficulty in gaining ingress to the palace, for the guards, some of them late from Komatzu, recognized him, and thought him possibly still a member of the household. It was late afternoon when he walked with down-bent head along the broad and gravelled pathway which led to the green lawn of the palace Nijo.

It was two months since Junzo had left his home in Kamakura, and, following the cortège of Princess Sado-ko, had come to Tokyo. There, during this time, he had wandered aimlessly about the city, trying to conquer the mad longing within him to see once again this princess. But his passion was stronger than himself, and now it had mastered him.

A servant, clad in modern livery, smiled behind his hand as the artist slipped his shoes off at the door; but Junzo, usually so quick to take offence at insolence, did not notice this new disdain of an old and honorable habit. He handed a letter and his card to the attendant, who, becoming more respectful, bowed his head to the level of Junzo's knees and ushered him with ceremony into a reception room.

The artist did not see the odd furnishing of the room, the plush upholstered chairs, the cabinets, the pictures in heavy gilt frames nailed to the light frame of shoji walls. His head bowed, his hands clasped behind him, Junzo walked up and down the apartment, while through his soul coursed the longing of his letter.

"Sado-ko! I will not call you princess, for this you have commanded me I must not do. I will call you Sado-ko—sweet Sado-ko! I come a mendicant to your august father's house, hungering for the sight of your dear face. I famish for the touch of your beloved hands, and cannot live for longing for your voice. And so, in beggar-wise, I come, beseeching you to see me for the space of one short hour again, to speak to me, to let me touch the hem of your kimono. Or if I ask too much, my Sado-ko, then let me once but look upon your face again, even though I may not speak to you, nor hear your voice. That night when, in the bamboo grove, we kept the tryst, I watched you pass from out my life with one whose name I cannot even write. The blackness of my fate closed down upon me then, blinding me to all light of earth or sky. For days, for nights, I wandered about the streets of Tokyo. I could not eat, nor sleep, nor think. I barely lived. My brain was scorched with but one name— my Sado-ko, my lotos maiden, my goddess of the sun! My father sent to seek me in the capital. But I was waiting there for you. Then rumor somehow pierced the gloom of my dark mind. It was said that you had gone to Kamakura, and would not come to Tokyo. It was my own dear home as well, and there I hastened, Sado-ko. They thought—my parents—that I came home at their solicitation. But no! I wandered by your palace walls. My fevered mind dreamed only of the time when chance might give me passing sight of you. Then one black night I heard you journeying from out the gate. I touched your norimono, and in the night I cried your name aloud; but, oh, alas! though I would have heard a whisper from your lips, you did not answer me—you made no sign, O Princess! Since then, in bitterness of spirit, I have lingered here in Tokyo, sometimes with harsh thoughts upon our love, but longing all the time for sight of you—for one small glimpse! 'As beat the restless waves on Biwa's strand,' so does my heart break for Sado-ko!"

A maid of honor, holding her long silken train across her arm, came down the wide stairway (a modern importation) of the Nijo palace, trailed her noisy skirt of taffeta across the hall, and paused within the doorway of the reception room.

She stood a moment without speaking, staring with baleful eyes at the bent head of the artist. Then she spoke softly, and with clearness.

"Good day, Sir Artist. It is an unexpected pleasure to see once more your august countenance."

Junzo turned his melancholy eyes upon her mocking face. Painfully he bowed, feeling in small mood to perform the courtesies of life.

"You are in excellent health, I trust?" she asked.

He bowed in answer. She smiled, and went a step nearer to him.

"I also hope you are still painting pictures just so fine as—"

She laughed derisively, and slowly, languidly unfurled her fan, a monstrous pinky thing of ostrich feathers.

A slow, dull flush grew upward in the face of Junzo. He did not deign to answer the taunting of the Lady Fuji-no.

"How is it, may I ask," she continued, "that you so cruelly deserted us upon our journey to the capital? It was declared about the court that you had been engaged by Prince Komatzu to execute a speaking likeness—such as was the one of Princess Sado-ko—of all the ladies of our court."

"Lady," said Junzo, with a certain scorn within his voice, which caused his tormentor to blush with angry shame, "I am not here to visit you. You do me honor in your unsought speech with me. Yet, I pray you, do not waste your wise and witty words upon a simple artist."

"Your words are rough, Sir Artist," she replied, her small eyes flashing, "yet though you state you did not come to visit me, you are perhaps mistaken. I am a maid of honor to her Highness Princess Sado-ko, and in my keeping she has condescended to intrust an answer to your letter."

He stared at her in shocked amazement.

"Through *you!*" he cried. "The Princess Sado-ko sent word by you?"

"Just so," she answered haughtily; "and so I trust you will guard your tongue in your words to one who is the august messenger of Princess Sado-ko."

"Give me her letter then," the artist said in a husky voice.

She laughed lightly.

"It is within my head, not hands, Sir Artist. The princess bade me state that she will condescend to grant your wish this evening. There will be a special ball within the palace, for his Majesty has sent his son, the young Crown Prince, but lately come of age, as guest to Nijo. The Princess Sado-ko bade me state you are invited."

She paused, watching with narrowed eyes the paling face of Junzo.

"For my part," she said, "I do not know the tenor of your letter, nor the request you dared to make of her Highness; but this I know, Sir Artist: to-night, if you accept this invitation, though you look at her with the keen eyes of love, you scarce will recognize your Princess Sado-ko."

"She is so changed?"

"So changed? Well, no and yes. Changed not in looks, artist, for beauty such as hers fades only with old age, but changed in ways, in action, speech, in very thought. You sighed, Sir Artist."

"You have keen ears," he said bitterly.

"Perhaps," she said, "your sighs will be much louder, artist, after you have seen her Highness. You will note the folly of illusions. You will not trace the change in Sado-ko to yourself, but to a master hand more royal."

"Lady, your words are veiled. I do not understand them."

"You will to-night. Had I more pity in my nature than the gods have given me, I could almost counsel just now: Stay in that dull world to which you rightfully belong and trust not all the words of Sado-ko. Nay, do not scowl. Your ancestors, I learn, were samurai. To-day you are a citizen—an artist-man. I am a lady of the court, cynical and little apt to trust my kind. Yet, artist, I think you will recall the words of Fuji when you are able to see with your own eyes the actions of her Highness with her new lover, the noble Prince Komatzu."

He spoke with sneering, cutting scorn:—

"Lady, your ambition ever trips before you. It is said you would gladly bring about the marriage of some noble persons for your own small ends. That union, I doubt not, will soon be consummated." He paled perceptibly even while he spoke the words, but continued with defiant bravery: "Yet do not waste your efforts in defaming to a poor artist one he trusts completely."

She brought her beaded slipper sharply down upon the floor.

"You speak the truth, Sir Artist. I would encompass such a union, and the gods favor my ambition. The Princess Sado-ko is kind to her affianced lord."

"They are not publicly betrothed," he said gloomily.

"Not yet, but the very coming of the Crown Prince indicates that the time is near. I will confess another weakness, artist. I do dislike your presence, and I fear it. If eyes and even ears are not deceived, the Princess Sado-ko loves her cousin Prince Komatzu."

He made a gesture of denial, but she continued steadily:—

"Yet by your coming I fear that older, wilder claims may reawake within the heart of the capricious princess."

"Her heart is steady as the sun," he said. "She is all nobleness and truth."

"You doubt that she has wavered toward her cousin?"

"I do not even think of it."

"So! You think the sex so true. Well, trust your eyes to-night, Sir Junzo!"

XX

AN EVIL OMEN

A rtist, you cannot enter the hall!" said the Duchess Aoi, pulling the sleeve of Junzo's hakama.

"I am a guest," he said briefly.

"But you transgress the most stringent rules of the court. His Majesty commands that no one, save in evening dress, shall appear. The Crown Prince is the guest of honor to-night."

Junzo looked with doubtful eyes at his dress, then stared at the black-coated, white-breasted garb of those within the room.

"It is the Prince of Nijo's palace; I am well aware that customs are changed here," he said.

"You think the Princess Sado-ko still sets the fashions at defiance. Oh, artist, she is a most abject devotee."

"I do not understand."

"Artist, for your own sake, do not look upon this new Sado-ko. Wait till the night is past, and see her in the morning. She will be then the princess you have known."

Both Junzo and the duchess started at a familiar sound of low, mocking laughter.

"What, dear Duchess Aoi, you deign to touch—to hold the sleeve of the honorable artist!" exclaimed the Lady Fuji-no.

Aoi's brown eyes flashed angrily.

"It was an honorable accident," she said haughtily. "I sought to save the artist from an error which would prove most humiliating to him. He is a stranger and does not know the rules as yet; but simply cast your eyes upon his dress, my lady, and you will see why I restrained him."

Fuji smiled in a superior, veiled way.

"Artist," she said, "Aoi is always thoughtful. She speaks the truth to-night. Pray heed her. If you step within the august hall, and even gaze at a great distance upon her Highness, you will lose your honorable head."

Junzo walked away from them and went upon the veranda of the palace. But Lady Fuji followed him. She pointed toward the long glass windows of the ball-room.

"Artist, the Duchess Aoi would prevent your seeing Sado-ko in her new garb. She clings to the despairing fancy that when her Highness sees you again, her feelings and also her dress will undergo a change, and that the old Sado-ko will once again bewitch the artist, and perchance save Komatzu for the Duchess Aoi."

"The duchess would prevent the marriage?" asked the artist, quietly.

"She is fairly mad to do so, artist, while I am equally determined to have it so. Now to which of us do you choose to lend yourself as a weapon?"

"Lady," said Junzo, gravely, "there is a Western proverb: 'Between two evils, choose the lesser.' Tell me, which of you is the lesser evil?"

She shrugged her thin, bared shoulders.

"Frankly, I confess of the two evils, Aoi or Fuji, I do not know which is the worse."

Junzo frowned gloomily through the windows into the brightly lighted room, now quickly filling. A trumpet blast, full and clear, resounded somewhere in the palace.

"Who enters now?" asked Junzo.

"The noble Prince Komatzu. Note the change upon his face, artist. Love prints her fingers on one's countenance as clearly as can be."

"And who comes now?"

"Put close your face against the barbarian pane. You see quite plainly?"

"Quite so."

"Well, look your full, Sir Artist. It is the Princess Sado-ko who comes."

He saw a glittering, spangled gown, low of neck and long of train. So long, indeed, it was that she who wore it tripped within it, and often lifted it in awkward style. Little high-heeled French slippers were upon the feet. The artist's eyes turned from surveying her strange, gorgeous gown, to her face, and there for a long, horror-stricken moment they remained.

Her face was creamy tinted, the eyes long, the brows finely pencilled. Her tiny lips were tipped with rouge, while her rich, shining hair was crumpled in a strange and massed coiffure. Wisps of hair, not straight or silky, but crinkled and curled like the hair of the unintellectual races, strayed about the face and sometimes fell upon her eyes. Her head was held straightly and proudly, and she did not deign to look about her. Her long, bare neck was weighted down with pearls and other flashing gems. Long, sleek, black gloves shut out the beauty of her arms.

With eyes distended, Junzo gazed upon her, like one fascinated with some strange, gliding serpent. He did not hear the loud fanfare of trumpets signalling the entrance of the young Crown Prince, nor note the sudden reverent silence within, the ceasing of the stir of fans, the silencing of voice and movement. Through his bewildered mind he thought he heard the mocking laughter of the Lady Fuji-no. Then suddenly the band crashed out, and the imperial ball had opened.

Slowly the artist turned, and in the light streaming from the window he gazed at the soft, smiling face of Fuji.

"It was a dream," he said, passing his hand across his brow.

"Awake, Sir Artist!" said the lady, "I trust you are already disillusioned."

He walked awhile up and down the veranda, then returned to her.

"Lady, the Duchess Aoi spoke truth. It was an order of the Emperor. She could not disobey. She is a martyr to the times."

"So! So!"

"So I believe," said Junzo, with unfaltering faith.

"You find her changed, then?"

"In dress—in garb, that is all."

"You did not see her face when she had deigned to turn it to the Prince Komatzu?"

"Beauty like hers will shine from very graciousness, my lady."

"Artist, as you are aware, the Princess Sado-ko is unconventional. To-night when the first ceremonies are past, she will leave this ballroom. She may not dance, being a princess royal. So she will retire to her private gardens, and there, I doubt not, will linger for a little while. Come with me there, and if she chance to see you, perhaps she will condescend to speak to you to-night. The princess but attends the ceremonials on these occasions. Hence we will not have to wait for long."

"A happy thought," he said eagerly, as he followed Fuji-no with willing feet.

It was dark without. The gardens in their modern dress lacked the charm of those of the palace Komatzu, yet Junzo trusted it would be different when they should come to Sado-ko's own private place. But here a disagreeable surprise awaited him. The place was in a state of great disorder, and the long reflection of the palace lights showed that the gardens were being changed in form and style.

"Follow me with care," said Fuji-no, "for as you see, the gardens of her Highness are undergoing change. Those who work by day are not so careful to render the place safe for evening loitering."

They came now to a new wing of the palace, which, too, appeared to be in process of alteration. The artist and the lady now paused to look about them. They heard a sound of fluttering movement close at hand. Junzo looked toward the balcony of the wing, from whence the odd movement proceeded.

"It is the royal nightingale," said Fuji, carelessly. "The foolish bird is beating out its life."

"The nightingale, my lady!"

"Yes. Have you never heard of the bird? It is the Princess Sado-ko's, a gift to her from his Majesty."

"I have heard of it," said Junzo, huskily.

Lady Fuji-no suppressed a yawn behind her fan, then turned impatiently toward the balcony whence came the ceaseless sound of the bird's movement.

"It is ill?" asked Junzo, shivering at those dumb signals of distress.

"Why, no—yes—you might so call it."

"How sad it must be for the princess," he murmured. "She loved the bird as though it were a human thing."

The Lady Fuji curled her scornful lip.

"Talk not, artist, of love in the same breath with Sado-ko. If it is love to cage a helpless thing—"

"Caged, you say! I do not understand. I was informed the cage was open always, but that the bird clung to it in very gratitude for the royal kindness shown."

"So it seemed till lately," said Fuji. "The princess, however, has been given to the most inexplicable whims and caprices, one of which was to close tight the door of her own nightingale, making it a prisoner. Since then the foolish thing seems ill and languishing, and spends the night in vain attempts to escape."

Junzo glanced uneasily toward the balcony. A moonbeam shone upon the gilded cage, depending from an eave by its long chain. The artist shuddered and paced restlessly about the path. Suddenly he came back to Fuji. His voice had a despairing note within it.

"Why did she do it, lady? Do you know the reason?" he asked.

"Do what, Sir Artist?"

"Cage up the bird, when it was hers already, captive to her will to come or go."

"A mere caprice, artist. One day she made a sudden exclamation of delight as though she had but just perceived the nightingale for the first time. 'Oh, see the joyous, pretty bird!' she said, 'and hear it sing!' It was at this time upon a camphor tree close by, and singing, in its own free way, a serenade no doubt to her. 'Why,' said the Countess Matsuka, ''tis your own nightingale, your Highness.' 'Mine!' said she, and seemed to pause bewilderedly. Then suddenly she clapped her hands. 'Oh, yes, for sure it is mine. Where is its cage?' 'Why, here,' said Countess Matsuka, who at this time alone attended her. The princess put her hand upon the cage, then, leaning from her balcony, chirped and whistled for the bird in such an odd and unfamiliar fashion that the countess was amazed, and still more so seemed the bird, for, pausing in its song, it cocked its head, fluttered its wings in sudden agitation, and then it spread them wide and flew away. The princess was so disappointed she wept in childish anger, though Countess Matsuka assured her it would return at dark, and take its night perch in the cage. 'And will it stay?' asked Sado-ko. 'Why, princess, just as ever.' Then she said she would not trust the bird, and on that very night, waited in person for its coming. With her own royal hands she trapped it in the cage and closed the door, though it was said her maiden, Natsu-no, implored her on her knees to spare it. Since then the maiden scarcely speaks, and like the bird is said to droop."

The artist smothered a deep groan.

"Do you not like the story?" asked the lady.

"I cannot believe it," he replied.

"Then look upon the cage yourself."

"It hurts my sight. I will not," said the man, and then he added, deeply, "It is an evil omen."

"Heed it, artist!" said the Lady Fuji-no.

XXI

"You are not Sado-ko!"

It was such another moonlight night as that on which the Princess Sado-ko kept her last tryst with the artist Junzo, but in the Nijo gardens no sight was reminiscent of the flowering gardens of Komatzu. No bamboo grove offered inviting lanes for loitering lovers, no stately camphor trees threw their flickering shadows of mystery upon the moonlit grass.

The lawns about the palace Nijo were quite bare of trees, and even by the wing of the Princess Sado-ko's apartments the new and ruthless carpenters, not gardeners, had torn up the bright flowering trees and shrubs to put in their places painted boxes, filled with foreign ferns and flowers of priceless value,—gifts from diplomats to the flattered Japanese.

Junzo and Fuji-no kept within the shadow of the princess's balcony, there being no trees or foliage at hand to screen them otherwise.

The new-laid path which led from the front of the palace to Sado-ko's wing, was white in the moonlight, hence Junzo was quick to see a shadow fall upon it. He leaned so far forward to gaze along the path, that Lady Fuji drew him backward.

"The light is on your head. Be careful, artist, if you please. Pray have some patience. They are quite close at hand."

Too close they seemed just then to Junzo, as they came along the broad, white path with slow and loitering steps. The tall soldier-prince bent to her who turned her face to his, like a flower to the sun.

When they had come quite close to Sado-ko's veranda they paused a moment, seeking some new excuse for lingering.

She made a childish movement, naïve yet eloquent. An artful shudder slipped her wrap to the ground. Her shining shoulders, bare and white, were revealed in the moonlight. The prince stooped quickly to the ground, picked up the cloak, and, hesitating a moment, held it in his hand. She shivered purposely. Then with a sudden movement he wrapped the cloak around her, and somehow in the doing his arms stayed for a space about her. Her face was close to his. Softly her loosened hair brushed now against his lips. While still his lingering arm was drooping on her shoulder, she said, in a low, wooing voice:—

"Komatzu, pray you hold my garment on me for a space, for I would take these long and stupid gloves from my arms."

"Let me do so," he begged eagerly; and, taking one of her small hands in his, slowly drew the glove away, then still held the hand clasped in his own.

"It is my hand—all mine!" he whispered. Stooping, he kissed the soft, white flesh, in the emotional French way.

"All yours, Komatzu!" Junzo heard her sigh in answer. The artist did not move. Like a man turned suddenly to stone, he simply stared out at the scene, with fixed eyes. He heard as in a dream the voice of this proud prince whispering again to her, who but so lately clung to him, the lowly artist, with such piteous tears and prayers.

"To-morrow," said the prince, "his Majesty will come to Tokyo. I will present myself before him and importune him to seal our betrothal. His ministers are all in favor of my suit, but the sanction of his Majesty is needed. That, I am sure, he intends to give, for I have heard that he made promise to our august grandmother, the Empress Dowager, that he would make sweet Sado-ko the highest princess in the land. Next to the Crown Prince of Japan, I am the highest prince."

She smoothed with little restless hand the foreign fabric of his coat. Her voice was somewhat faint:—

"If his Majesty should not consent, Komatzu?"

"Why even dream of such a thing?" he asked. "Am I not the very one most fitted for your husband, and have I not served well his Majesty?"

She seized his hand and held it close against her face.

"Komatzu, were I not of equal rank with you,—if I were but a simple maiden of humble parentage,—would you still love me?"

"I do not love your rank, sweet cousin, but your own self."

"But if I were not of your rank, what then?"

"Capricious Sado-ko, why ask such foolish questions?"

"Would you still marry me if I were not a royal princess?"

"I still would love you, Sado-ko. I could not marry you in that event. Why, you turn your face away! The tears are in your eyes. Cousin, you are too fanciful."

"Love makes me so," she said, and sighed.

"How strange," he said, "that we should speak so freely of our love. A little while ago the subject would have been deemed indecent. Now it is a foreign fashion and we Japanese speak out our love without the smallest blush of shame. 'Tis strange, indeed!"

"It is not only fashion," she protested; "love is not a new thing,—a caprice, a whim, like such and such a dress, a hat or shoe or fan."

"It is a new device of speech in our Japan," the prince declared, thoughtfully.

With childish petulance she turned toward the balcony.

"Which you do not approve, Komatzu?"

"Why, yes, I do approve it, Sado-ko. It is most beautiful and pure, moreover. But, cousin, as you know, I never spoke it yet—this love—till lately. Then, somehow, when you came back from the palace Aoyama, a something in your eyes seemed to beckon me to you and force the words of love to overrun my lips."

"They were not merely words of lips?"

"No, no. But I, you know, am not completely modern in my thought, despite my dress, and, too, I am a soldier. So sometimes if my words seem clumsy—stupid—I fear you must compare them with the flowery speeches of others."

"Others, Komatzu? What others could there be?"

His voice was low and nervous. He seemed to hesitate.

"Cousin, have you forgotten the artist-man?"

"The artist-man!" she gave a little cry, then quickly covered up her lips with her fingers.

"You start! Kamura Junzo his name was. Once I thought you favored him. So thought all the members of the court. I could not close my ears against the romance, though I severely disapproved the slander, and named it such; for I deemed your condescension to the man the idle fancy of a princess noted for her oddities and caprices. But lately, the mere thought of him causes my brain to burn with raging and unworthy jealousy."

She rested one small hand against the railing of her balcony, then slowly drew up her slender figure.

"The artist is no more to me," she said, "than any slave who dresses me, sings to me, entertains me, comes at my command, or paints for me my picture."

"Yet, Sado-ko, the artist did not paint your picture."

For a moment she stood still in bewilderment, then went a step toward him. Her words were stammering, then changed to fervent, passionate appeal.

"Why, yes, he painted—that—assuredly he painted—it does not matter what the artist did. Komatzu, I have no thought within my mind, nor love within my heart, for any one in all the world save you."

He took her hands and drew them upward to his lips, there to hold them for a space, then let them go again.

"I am quite satisfied," he said. "Truth itself shines in your face, my Sado-ko. And now, sweet cousin, we will say good night, for it is late, and I would not have your beauteous eyes lose one small atom of their lustre. And so for the night, sayonara!"

Softly and lingeringly she repeated the word. She watched him as he walked along the path, until he had quite disappeared. Then slowly, dreamily she ascended the little steps. She stopped in sudden irritation at the sound of the restless bird within the cage. Moving toward it, she shook the cage with some nervous violence.

"Be still!" she said. "You break my thoughts, you foolish bird! Be still, I say!"

The Lady Fuji touched the artist's arm. He did not stir. Peering up into his face, she started back at sight of the dull, frozen look. A glimmer of compassion crossed her breast. She whispered:—

"Artist, come away."

He did not move.

"Pray come!" urged Fuji.

Masago, standing by the bird-cage on the balcony, thought she heard some whispering voices close at hand. She leaned over the railing and called, in fearful voice:—

"Who are the honorable ones below?"

As Fuji sought to draw the artist away, the movement of her effort reached the ears of her mistress. The latter crossed the veranda with quick steps, and, leaning down close to the sound, saw those two figures in the shadow. A moment later the Lady Fuji-no, drawing her cape before her face, fled along the path, and disappeared.

Moving mechanically to the light, the artist turned his face to Masago. A muffled cry escaped her lips. She shrank back, still clinging to the railing of the balcony.

"Kamura Junzo!" she cried. "You!—and here!"

"I do not know your voice," he said in strange, wondering tones.

"I remember now," she said. "You wrote a letter to the Princess Sado-ko. You wished to look—look at her. You—you asked the favor. Well—I—I am Sado-ko!"

He moved his head and stared upon her face with straining eyes.

"You are not Sado-ko!" he said.

She trembled with fear.

"I do assure you"—she began, her hand going to her throat to stay her frightened breathing.

"You are not Sado-ko, I say!"

Her voice was raised and shrill.

"I am the Princess Sado-ko," she cried. "I do defy you, artist-man, to prove I am not Sado-ko."

His vague and wandering words recalled her self-possession. She knew that she had needlessly excited her fears.

"You are not Sado-ko," he said, "for she was kind and sweet; but you—you are a nightmare of my Sado-ko. Your face is hers, yet still you are not Sado-ko. Your soul is false; your heart is dead, for Sado-ko is dead, and you who once were Sado-ko are but her ghost. You are not Sado-ko."

She grew afraid of that white, glaring face, and hoarse, wandering voice. Turning, she hastened to her room, drawing the doors close behind her.

The artist stood alone. Then suddenly he laughed out wildly, loudly. Again he paused in silence. Then laughed aloud again, in that wild way. He heard the noise, the heavy step of palace guards. Then Junzo turned and fled like the wind, his fleet and sandalled feet carrying him with more than natural speed onward and onward. Past startled groups of garden revellers, past loitering lovers, and past guards about the grounds, and outward through the palace gates he plunged on toward the city, gleaming out in specks of light below.

XXII

The Coming Home of Junzo

Though samurai by birth, the Kamura family were of gentler nature than their stern ancestors, and so no feeling of anger or bitterness had been cherished against their son Junzo. His parents made their sad apologies to their guests, who hastily departed, cloaking their feelings behind their well-bred, stoic faces. Yamada Kwacho alone lingered to speak a word of gruff sympathy to the parents, and to offer what aid was in his power. When they insisted that their son was surely ill, Kwacho said at once he would go to Tokyo and personally seek the young man in the capital.

Meanwhile, the Kamura family kept a tireless, ceaseless watch for Junzo. Though days and weeks and then a month slipped slowly by, each member of the household took his place by day at a small lookout station to watch for any sight of ani-san (elder brother). By night a light turned to the east burned at the casement of Junzo's chamber, while mother and father knelt at shoji doors, keeping the watch. Thus would they watch by day and night, so any hour he might come would find them waiting patiently.

Two months had passed since Junzo left Kamakura, when the belated word came from Tokyo. Yamada Kwacho had found the wandering Junzo.

No member of the Kamura family retired that night. Even the smallest child knelt by the shoji and watched for Junzo. A series of heavy rains had darkened the days and nights. The clinging fog of the Hayama hung heavily in the atmosphere.

Not a star or gleam of moon shone out to soften the blackness of the night sky. When the slothful morning crept in timid wonder over the hills, and pushed with soft, gray hands the night away, the watchers saw the fog was vanquished, and that the pale morning mist bespoke a brighter day to dawn.

When the first gleam of the long-looked-for sun came up the eastern slope, Junzo staggered down the hills of Kamakura toward his home. Those watching at the shoji saw him as he passed with down-bent head within the gate. Then the calm of caste and school broke down before the throb of parenthood. Father and mother hastened down the garden path to meet their son.

"The fog!" It was the mother who spoke in sobbing tones, as she fondled the hands of her eldest son. "You honorably did lose your way, Junzo."

His restless eyes wandered from hers, and he pushed back, absently, the long black locks that tumbled on his brow.

"It was the fog that kept you, Junzo?" she urged.

"The fog?" he said dazedly. "No—that is, yes. It was the fog, good mother."

"So dark at night! Oh, son, we thought that you might wander from the path and come to the river bank." She shuddered at the thought.

"Yet, you came down from the direction of the hills," said his father, anxiously. "Did you abide there last night?"

"Yes," said Junzo, "throughout the long, long night, my father."

The silent Kwacho shook his head, then whispered in the father's ear:—

"We arrived last night, good friend, quite early, but Junzo, as you see, is ill and I could not leave him for a moment. Hence, Oka being nowhere at hand, and not a vehicle in sight, I sought to lead him homeward. But no, he turned his feet in new directions. He stumbled here and there across the fields and up and down the hills, and finally we reached the walls of Aoyama. I could not lead him, since he would not have it so, and so I humored his strange fancy, and hence, good friend, have spent the night crouched down beside the palace walls, without covering, indeed, without the much-desired good sleep."

"Oh, come indoors, at once," the mother entreated, for Junzo lingered absently on the threshold. "Your face is pale, dear son, and oh, your clothes are quite soaked with dew."

He followed her mechanically, though he seemed, as yet, to have noted nothing of the haggard aspect of their loving faces. His thoughts seemed far away. When his youngest brother, a little boy of five, came with running steps to meet him and called his name, he simply tapped the child upon the head.

The anxious mother had now become the zealous nurse and housewife. She clapped her hands a dozen times, and sent two attendants speeding for warm tea and dry clothes. The children were put in charge of Haruno, who took them immediately to a neighbor's house. Soon there was no one left in the apartment save mother and son.

"We will take good care of you, my son," she said, "and when you are quite recovered, we will have another council."

He repeated the word stupidly.

"Of what council do you speak?"

She stroked the damp hair backward with her tender fingers.

"My Junzo always was the absent-minded son, so given to his studies and his art he could not spare a thought for other matters."

He put his hands upon those on his head, and drew his mother about until she was before him. Then, looking in her face with searching, troubled eyes, he said:—

"Was there a council of our family?"

"Why, yes, my son,—that day you went to Tokyo."

He passed his hand across his brow, then seemed to listen for a space. Slowly a look of horror crept across his face.

"It was my marriage council!" he gasped.

"Why, yes, dear Junzo; your marriage to the maid Masago. Ah, you are quite ill, my son."

He sprang to his feet, and stood in quivering thought. She heard him mutter half aloud, despairingly:—

"But she had gone away—to Tokyo. They told me so."

"Why, no, it is a mistake. Who told you that she went to Tokyo, my son?"

"The palace guards," he said, not looking at his mother.

"Oh, you are surely ill, my son."

"I am not ill," he said, with persistent gentleness; "but I am speaking truth, dear mother. Do I not know of what I speak, for was I not close by the palace walls throughout the length of one whole night? I tell you, mother, that I *saw* her go to Tokyo."

His mother threw her arms about his neck, then, bursting into tears, clung to him.

"Son," she sobbed, "do not speak of Tokyo. The parent of your fiancée, Yamada Kwacho, is even now within our domicile, and the chaste maiden is safe in her home."

He spoke with slow and hazy positiveness:—

"She went to Tokyo that night. I was so close unto her norimon that I could even touch it, and through the fog and the dim night I cried her name aloud. It sounded wildly in the night air."

He undid the clinging arms about his neck, and stood as though plunged deep in moody thought. When his father and brother came into the room, he did not lift his head.

"Junzo, do you know your brother?" asked the youth Okido, stepping to his side.

Junzo raised his head.

"Why, yes, you are my younger brother, Kido-sama. Good morning!"

"Oh, ani-san!" cried the youth, in mournful tones. "How strangely you speak, how strangely you look!"

"Son," said the father, sternly, laying his hands on Junzo's shoulder, "it is your father speaking now. I named you Junzo (obedience). From youth you have obeyed my voice. Now come! I bid you go to your chamber. There you shall lie, your mother and young sister will attend you, and Kido here shall hasten for a learned doctor, a foreign man of science lately come to Kamakura. You are distraught and ill."

"But I am well, most honored parent."

"I say that you are ill."

"I am quite well, excellent father, and I must go at once to Tokyo."

"I command obedience to my will! Come, Junzo!"

"Command! A little while ago—or maybe it was long ago, within another lifetime, she said it was an ancient practice to obey parental command. Yet I always was so fond of the old rules of life that I will recognize my duty, father. I bow in filial submissiveness to your high will."

But as he bowed his head in mock obedience he was so weak he would have fallen down, but that the sturdy Kido and his father supported him.

For days and weeks the artist-man of Kamakura tossed upon a bed of illness, a prey to violent fever of the brain, so termed by the great Dutch doctor visiting the little town. After many days there came a calm. Junzo slept and dreamed.

He thought the angel face of Sado-ko bent over his heated head, and that she brushed the tumbled locks back from his brow, and cooled it with her own soft, lovely hands. He cried her name and whispered it again and yet again. Was it only fancy, or did he truly hear that low, low voice, sighing back in answer, and soothing him with tender words of love?

ONOTO WATANNA

XXIII

THE CONVALESCENT

It was a happy day in the Kamura household when the cheerful and rapid-moving foreign doctor pronounced the patient strong enough to leave his room to sit a little while upon the balcony. His brothers were eager to assist the weak and emaciated Junzo to the soft seat they had prepared for him. He protested that he was able to walk alone, but finally admitted that the light, guiding hand of his fiancée was a sufficient support.

So leading him with careful step, the young girl aided her lover, while all his brothers, and his young sister Haru-no, watched the pretty picture with moistened eyes. The gentle mother slipped from the room to weep alone at what she called "the goodness of the gods."

Once upon the balcony, the modest maiden quickly bent her head over her embroidery frame, feigning ignorance of the eyes upon her. While the convalescent absently answered the questions of his brothers, concerning his comfort, his eyes scarcely left the face of the quiet girl so close at hand.

A certain wistful wonder seemed to lurk within the eyes of Junzo in these days. Yet a sense of rest and quiet pervaded his whole being. His lately racked heart and mind seemed to have found a strange, sustaining balm.

Now on this lovely day in early September, with the odor of the gardens permeating the atmosphere, and the sweet breath of the country about, Junzo's mind went vaguely over the late events of his life, while his eyes rested in wondering content upon the drooped face of his fiancée.

The artist, in his illness, had been attended by one he called "Sado-ko." When fever left him and partial sense and reason crept back to his weakened brain, growing daily with the strength of his physical body, he marvelled over that exquisite face that bent above him.

And then one day his sister, Haru-no, had called her by name— Masago! A light broke through the dazzled brain of Junzo. She who nursed him with tender care was not a princess, but a simple maiden of his own class, and, most marvellous, she was his own betrothed, the virtuous maid Masago! Reason was restored, and physical strength increased daily.

Through the many days when he was forced to obey the will of the insistent foreign doctor, Junzo did not fret at his enforced confinement. Such an existence was fraught with dreamful possibilities of happiness. As Junzo's thoughts became clear, this was his solution of what he termed his recent madness: He had loved Masago from the first, he told himself. The very gods had planned their union. Before he had known fully the heart of his betrothed, she was sent away to school. By chance this Princess Sado-ko crossed his path, the image of the maid Masago. It was because of this he had thought he loved her, while it was the other he loved. This was proved by the fact that with a lover's adoration he was now drawn to Masago.

These were the thoughts of Junzo. Still more curious was his way of comparing the princess and the maiden, with a weight of favor for the latter. In her constant presence Junzo thought darkly of the falsity of Sado-ko, and with ecstasy of the charming simplicity of this girl of lowly birth.

As she sat with her pretty head dropped over her work, he thought her lovelier than ever he had dreamed the Princess Sado-ko.

Once during the afternoon his relatives left the two alone. Then the girl softly raised her eyes, to glance in his direction. At the ardent glance she met, her eyes dropped immediately. So much did he wish to see again those dark and lovely eyes that he complained of a discomfort.

He desired another quilt (though it was very warm), and also a high futon for his head. She brought them to him, without speaking. When she put the pillow underneath his head, he tried to speak her name with all the ardor of his love.

"Sado—" He stopped aghast. His lips had framed that other name. The kneeling maiden's eyes met his. Her voice was soft:—

"Who is Sado-ko?" she asked.

Flushing in shame and mortification, he could not meet her eyes. When she repeated her quiet question, the strangest smile dimpled her lips at the frown upon his averted face.

"Who is Sado-ko?"

"It is a name," he said, "just a name."

"It has a pretty sound," she said.

Though he moved his head restlessly, she pursued the subject.

"Do you not think so, Junzo?"

"It is an evil name," he said with sudden vehemence. Although he did not see the little movement of dismay she made, he knew that she was leaning toward him. He could not look at her.

"You do not like the name of Sado-ko?" she said. "Why, that is strange!"

At last he looked at her, then wondered why she swiftly blushed, averting her eyes.

"Why strange?" he asked, his eyes lingering upon her flushing face.

"Because it was a name you called unceasingly throughout your illness," she said.

"I called on you." He took her hand to hold it closely within his own.

She stammered over her words, thrilling at his touch upon her hands.

"But is my—my name, then—Sado-ko?" she asked.

His troubled eyes were on her face, a wistful wonder in their glance.

"I thought you so," he whispered softly.

She let her hand remain in his, for it was sweet to feel his touch, yet, with the strangest stubbornness, she urged the question:—

"Why did you think me Sado-ko?"

"I will tell you why some other day," he answered in a low voice.

"But am I not Masago?" she persisted.

"Yes," said he, "Masago is your name, and it is sweeter, simpler, lovelier far than—"

She drew her hands from his with passionate petulance. Her eyes were hurt.

"You like Masago better, then, than Sado-ko?" was her astonishing question.

"The name? Why, yes. It has a sweeter sound—Masago! 'Tis the loveliest of flowers,—modest, simple, and fair."

She caught her breath. When she raised her eyes to his, they were full of deep reproach. Moving away she turned her back, and would not turn or listen to his calling of her name:—

"Masago, Masago!" Then, after a short silence, "Have I offended you, Masago?"

She answered without turning her head:—

"You have offended Sado-ko."

He could not answer that strange, inexplicable remark, so kept silent for a space. Then:

"Masago, pray you turn your pretty head this way."

She moved it petulantly.

He raised himself upon his elbow.

"Masago!"

She did not answer.

"Well, then, if you will treat me so, and will not come to me like a most dutiful affianced wife, why I, though ill, shall come to you." He made a threatening stir. At that she started toward him, anxiety for his health stronger than her childish petulance.

"No, no, do not move," she said. "I—I will come to you if—if you desire it."

She took her place again by his side. Immediately he possessed himself of both her slim hands.

"Now look at me," he said.

She met his eyes, then flushed and trembled at the love she must have seen reflected in his face.

"Masago," he said, "when Junzo once again regains his normal strength, he has a tale to tell his little wife,—a foolish tale of youth's brief madness in a summer, of heart-burning and heart-breaking, tears of weakness, filial disobedience, falsity, and then—despair. Afterward—the light!"

"The light?" she said in a strange, breathless voice.

"A face," he said,—"the soothing face of my Masago."

"Oh, do not call me so," she cried almost piteously; "I cannot bear to hear it."

"Why—"

"Call me not Masago. I do not like the name."

"But—"

"No, no. It is quite well that others—say my honorable parents and brothers—should call me so, but it sounds unkindly from your lips, dear Junzo. Indeed, I—I hardly can express my feelings. I—I—"

She broke off at the expression of bewilderment upon his face. Nervously she entangled her fingers.

"Call me what you will. Let it be Masago, if the name pleases you. There! my foolish mood is past. I am your gentle girl once more."

"I will not call you by your name," he said, smiling whimsically, "since you do not like it. In a little while I'll have another, sweeter name for you—wife!"

XXIV

A Royal Proclamation

In the palace Nijo the latest royal proclamation came like an earthquake shock. The Emperor at last had kept his word to his dead mother. Through word to Nijo, he authorized the nuptials of the Princess Sado-ko to his own son, the Crown Prince of Japan, thus elevating her to the highest position in the land.

This great fortune, sudden and unexpected, gave no satisfaction to the ambitious Masago. The test of life had come. The woman in her triumphed. For the first time since her coming to Tokyo, Masago shut herself alone within the chamber of the Princess Sado-ko.

She sat and stared before her like one struck by so great a weight that she could not lift it. All her life she had longed for wealth and power. Now that the greatest honor in the land was forced upon her, she shrank from it, in loathing.

Masago thought with aching heart of the Prince Komatzu. Throughout the day she sat alone, uttering no word, not even answering the queries of her maid, the woman Natsu-no.

Toward evening she heard the palace bells ringing. Knowing why they rang, she pressed her hands to her ears, a sickening sense oppressing her. She heard the dim voice of the maid.

"Princess, will you deign to robe to-night?"

Slowly, mechanically, Masago arose, permitting the woman to lay upon her a foreign gown which only yesterday had come from Paris. Now its tightening stifled her. Her heavy breathing caused the woman to ask gently:—

"You do not appear augustly comfortable to-night, exalted princess. Are you quite well?"

Masago threw her bare arms above her head, and paced the floor like some tortured being. Suddenly she turned upon the woman, crying out in an hysterical way:—

"Why do you stand and stare at me, woman! Oh-h! My head is throbbing, and my heart beats so—"

She covered her face with her hands. Swiftly the woman withdrew. In the next room she took her stand by the dividing shoji, watching the one within.

"She would treat me like the bird," she said, "and it is dead."

Masago called her shrilly, harshly.

"Woman! Maid! Do you not hear me calling?"

"I am here, princess!" said the woman, quietly, stepping back into the room.

"I cannot bear this gown to-night," said Masago. "It suffocates me. It is ill-fitting."

The woman patiently removed the gown, then waited for her mistress to command her further.

"Take them all off," said the girl, in an irritated voice. "These and these."

She indicated the silk corsets and the frail shoes which gave her such unstable support. Freed of the foreign garments, she seemed to breathe with more ease and comfort.

"Now a kimono,—just a simple, plain one."

The woman brought the plainest one of all. Soon Masago was arrayed in this.

"Do I appear well to-night?" she asked hysterically.

"Yes, princess."

"Will not his Royal Highness be astonished at my garb?"

"Enchanted, princess."

"Enchanted! You speak foolish words! He is a modern prince, this future Emperor of Japan. He will despise a plain kimono."

The woman closed her lips.

"Say so," insisted the girl, wildly. "Agree with me, woman, that when he sees me in this garb to-night, he will detest the sight of me, and insist unto his father that he must have another bride. Oh, you do not speak! How I hate you!"

She was sobbing as she left the room in a breathless, piteous way, for no tears came to give relief.

Like one in a dream Masago passed through the halls of the Nijo palace. Soon she was in the great reception hall, where the Crown Prince, guest of her father, Nijo, awaited her appearance. Her courtesy was mechanical. She took her place beside him on the slight eminence reserved for royalty alone.

Masago little cared that night whether her maidens whispered and gossiped at her whim to appear once more in the national dress. It was suggested that she wore the gown in compliment to her exalted fiancée.

As the girl surveyed the brilliant spectacle, an intense weariness overtook her. Half unconsciously she closed her eyes and put her head back against the tall throne chair upon which she sat. Then Masago became deaf—blind to all about her. Strange visions of her home passed through her mind,—her simple home, quiet, peaceful. As in fancy she saw Ohano's sympathetic face, she felt an aching longing to hear her garrulous voice lowered to her in gossip; she saw again her happy, healthy little brothers, romping in the sunny garden. Even the thought of Kwacho, grave yet always just and kind, despite his narrow prejudices, awoke a vague tenderness.

When some one spoke the name of Princess Sado-ko, she roused herself, then shuddered at the very sound.

"You were so pale, princess, and you closed your eyes just now. I thought, perchance, that you were ill." The Crown Prince of Japan spoke with polite solicitude to the maid Masago. Her eyes filled with heavy tears.

"Oh, I am homesick—homesick!" she murmured in reply.

He leaned a trifle toward her, as though his boredom were lifted for a second.

"Are you not at home already, princess?"

She shook her head in mute negation.

"What do you call your home, then?" he inquired.

She answered in a whisper:—

"Kamakura!"

"Ah, yes, the castle Aoyama is there."

She could not speak further. A page brought tea on a small lacquered tray. She touched it with her lips, then again relapsed into her attitude of weariness and languor.

The Crown Prince thought his cousin both stupid and dull. He mentally decided that her beauty had been overrated. Bright, flashing eyes, rosy lips, a vivacious countenance, in these days were considered a more desirable type of beauty than this tired, languid, waxen sort, mysteriously sad, despite perfection.

He wondered whether her allusion to Kamakura had to do with the famous artist there, of whom the young prince had heard.

Report had told him that the capricious Sado-ko had treated this plain artist with familiarity such that the court gossiped. While these thoughts ran vaguely through his mind, the princess interrupted with a question:—

"When is the wedding-day?" she asked.

"It is not set," he replied somewhat stiffly.

Her hands moved restlessly in her lap.

"Are there not other ladies of the royal house more exalted than I?" she asked.

"None, illustrious princess," he answered coldly.

She turned her miserable face aside, and stared at the company with eyes that would fill with tears. Suddenly, hardly conscious of her words, she exclaimed, in a low, passionate voice:—

"I hate it all! I hate it all!"

The Crown Prince stared in astonishment at her feverishly flushed face.

"I overheard your words, princess," he said, with forbidding candor. "I do not know to what you are alluding. The words themselves have an unseemly sound."

She pressed her lips together, and sat in bitter silence after that. Suddenly she became conscious of compelling eyes upon her. She moved and breathed with a new excitement. Then she heard the Crown Prince speaking in a sarcastic, drawling way, which already she had begun to dislike.

"Our cousin, here, Komatzu, is sick for Kamakura."

She turned her helpless eyes upon Komatzu's face. To her passionate, hungry eyes he appeared impassive and unmoved. Had the horrible tidings, then, left him only cold? Were the words of love he had whispered so often in her ear but the carefully prepared words of a formal suitor? Was he so much a prince that he could mask his heart behind so impenetrable a countenance?

Tears, welling up from her aching heart, dropped unheeded from her eyes. She made no effort to wipe them away, or to conceal her childish grief and agony. So this lately elevated princess, affianced to a future emperor, sat by his side in a public place, with tears running down her face. The Crown Prince was impatient at this display of weak emotion, she knew, and her action was unbefitting a princess of Japan; nevertheless she found herself repeating over and over again in her heart:—

"I am not a princess! I am not a princess! I am only the maid Masago. That is all. I have been but playing at a masquerade, and I am tired. I want my home—my parents. My heart is breaking!"

XXV

The Eve of a Wedding

It was the month of Kikuzuki (Chrysanthemum). Summer was dying,—not dead,—and in her latter moments her beauty was ethereal, though passionate. The leaves were brown and red. The grass was warmer colored than at any other time of year. The glorious chrysanthemum, queen of all the flowers in Japan, lent golden color to the landscape. The skies were deeply blue. Sometimes, when the sinking sun was slow in fading, its ruddy tints upon the blue made of the heavens a purple canopy, enchanting to the sight. Yet with all its beauty November is the month of tears, for Death, however beautiful, must always wring the heart. So lovers are pensive and melancholy in their happiness at this sweet, sad season of the year.

It was the eve before the wedding of the artist and the maid Masago. Junzo's artful insistence that he was not strong enough to do without the helpful nursing of his fiancée had kept her for many days a guest within his father's house. Now it wanted but the passing of one night before the day when the wedding would take place at the house of Kwacho. Hence the lovers were on their way from the Kamura residence. It was twilight. The two loitered in their steps along the way, pausing on every excuse within the woods, the meadow fields, and even on the open highway. They spoke but little to each other, and then only at intervals. But when they had approached quite near the house, the girl said tremulously:—

"When we are married, Junzo, I want to make a little trip with you—alone."

"Where, Masago?"

She stopped, looking toward the hills. Then, with one hand on his arm and the other lifted from her sleeve, she pointed:—

"Look, Junzo, how the royal sun lingers on the palace turrets. It seems to love Aoyama."

Junzo surveyed the golden peaks of the palace, shining red in the sunset glow. His thoughts prevented speech. His mind dwelling on that one who had once made her home within the palace, he forced his eyes away to turn them on the dreamy face of his Masago.

"You spoke of a little trip, Masago. Where shall it be, then?"

"Yonder," she said, still pointing toward the palace.

His face was troubled.

"I do not understand. You do not mean—"

Slowly she nodded her head.

"Yes, I mean to Aoyama, just up there on the hills, my Junzo. It would be a little journey, and I—I want just once again in my life to loiter in the gardens."

"You have already been there, then?" he asked, with some astonishment.

She caught her breath, then simply bowed her head.

"I have been there in fancy, Junzo, or perhaps it was in dreams," was her reply. "Will you not go with me sometime, in fact?"

He hesitated, and moved uncomfortably.

"I do not understand your fancy," he said.

"Well, make the little journey with me, will you not?"

"The palace is not public property," he answered.

As she did not respond at once, he seized the opportunity to continue their walk, thinking in this way to divert her. It was growing softly darker. In the twilight her face was so ethereal and perfect that the artist could not take his eyes from it. Suddenly she said quite simply:—

"You have fame at court, and so you could obtain a pass to enter the grounds."

"Why, have you so strange a fancy, Masago?"

"Is it strange?" she asked, and stopped again. In the dusk of the woodland lane, her upturned face appeared timid, wistful.

"Yes, it is strange for a maiden of our class, Masago, to wish to enter royal gardens."

"Are they not beautiful?" she asked wistfully.

"Beautiful? Perhaps, to some eyes, but to my mind not of that more desirable beauty nature gives to our more simple gardens."

"Once you thought the gardens peerless," she said; "have you forgotten, Junzo?"

He started violently. Suddenly his hand fell upon her arm. In the dimly fading light he bent to see her face.

"How can you know of—Masago, your words are strange."

She laughed in that soft way so reminiscent to him always of that other one.

"They are not strange, indeed," she said, "for I have often heard that

ONOTO WATANNA

you declared the palace grounds were beautiful. But then," she sighed, and resumed the walk, "an artist is no less a man, and therefore fickle."

They did not speak again until they reached Yamada's house. At the little garden gate they paused.

"How quiet all the world seems to-night!" she said.

"You say that in a melancholy tone of voice, Masago."

"Yes, I am a little melancholy. It is the season and the night. Have you forgotten, Junzo, that to-morrow—"

He did not let her finish, but seized both her hands.

"How can you ask that question? I think of that to-morrow every second. To-night I will not sleep."

"Nor I," she said.

"What will you do? Tell me, sweet Masago, and I will engage the night in the same way."

She nestled against his arm, looking toward the stars.

"To-night," she said, "I'll sit beside my shoji doors and I will watch the moon. I'll tell my heart that I am keeping tryst with you, and think that it is so, that you and I, my Junzo, are alone in some sweet garden, keeping a moon tryst."

He dropped her hands. She could hear his quickened breath. In the shadow he could not see her face. How could he have guessed that Sado-ko was jealous of her very self?

"Why did you drop my hands?" she asked.

He seemed to be in painful thought. His voice was husky when he spoke:—

"Your words, Masago, start bitter recollections in my mind."

"Bitter?" she repeated softly.

"Bitter, bitter," he replied.

She broke his thought, with a timid question.

"Junzo, this is our wedding-eve. Confide in me."

He moved from her a step, and stood in indecisive silence. Then:—

"There is nothing to confide."

"You told me once there was a tale that you would tell me."

With an impetuous motion he once again seized her hands.

"You are too good, too pure to hear the story of one both false and base."

In the strangest, most piteous of voices she answered:—

"Perhaps there was another time when you called her by another name."

Her strange words rendered him quite speechless. She put her hand upon his arm. There was a pleading quality in her voice:—

"Junzo, do not think or speak unkindly of poor Sado-ko," she said.

He repeated the name in a low, despairing voice:—

"Sado-ko!"

The very name recalled his anguish of the past.

"You love her still?" she asked. Now a note of fear was in her voice. She could not bear that he should speak or think unkindly of the Princess Sado-ko, yet the very thought that he should love one who was no longer herself, rendered this paradox of women distracted.

"You love her still?" she asked, catching his arm and shaking it with her childish jealousy.

"No, no," he said, as though the very thought was loathsome, "'tis you alone I love, my own Masago."

Her tone was sharply tart.

"You do not love Sado-ko?"

"I love Masago," he said.

She sighed.

"I would not have it otherwise," she said, and laughed happily.

"Masago," he said earnestly, "ask the consent of your honored parent that I may come indoors. We will spend a portion of the night together. I will then tell you all you wish to know concerning that passion of the heart I once have felt, which you have suspected. It is better you should know."

XXVI

Masago's Return

Alone in the quiet guest room of the Yamada house they sat. Convention demanded a light, but it was of the dimmest—a dull and flickering andon. Yet the night was clear. By the shoji walls they sat, looking into each other's faces, thinking always of the morrow.

She had listened without interrupting while in low, tense voice he had told her of a madness once felt for a high princess. When he had quite finished and sat in silent, moody gloom, she moved nearer to him, then slipped her hand into his, and nestled up against his shoulder. Her voice was soothing in its quality.

"By this time the little bird—the poor caged nightingale is dead," she said. "The gods were more kind to you, Junzo, for see, you are so strong you beat away the cage-bars and are quite free to love again."

Pressing his face against her hair, he said solemnly:—

"The gods are witness of this fact. You are the only one that I have ever loved."

Smiling, she sighed with happiness.

"Poor Sado-ko!" she said.

His voice was earnest.

"I loved you in her, Masago."

She smiled in sweetest confidence now.

"That is true," she said. "I do believe it, and to-morrow—"

"To-morrow will be a golden day upon the august calendar of our lives. I love you! Men of our country do not always marry for their love, Masago, but the gods are kind, and favor us!"

"How sad," she said, "it must be to marry one for whom we do not care!"

"It is the fate of many in our land."

"The times change, Junzo-san. Are not conditions happier to-day?"

"True. In the years to come they will still improve, and if the gods grant us honorable offspring—"

"What is that?" she cried, starting from him suddenly. "I thought I heard one moving—and see, oh, look, there is a shadow on the shoji wall!"

"Where?"

"Over there! See, it is moving now. Some one is upon our balcony. Oh, Junzo!"

She clung to him in a shivering panic of fear.

"Do not tremble so, Masago. Some foolish listening servant, that is all! One moment, we will see!"

He started to cross the room to the opposite side, but she clung to him with nervous apprehension.

"No, no—I am fearful!" she whispered.

"But some one is without. I too saw and see the shadow of the form. Why should our simple courtship be spied upon? Let me see who it is, Masago?"

They were speaking in whispers. The girl was trembling with fright.

"It is an evil omen on this night," she whispered pitifully. "Do not, pray you, do not seek to find the cause."

"Your fear is most incomprehensible. Let us go to another room, then. We will join your honorable parents."

She clung to him fearfully as they made their way across the room together. The shadow on the shoji moved upward from its crouching position, and through the thin walls the lovers saw an arm, with the long sleeve of a woman falling from it, extended to push aside the doors.

Upon a sudden impulse Junzo strode toward the doors and opened them. The figure on the balcony stood still, silhouetted in the silvered light of the night. Between the parted shoji she stood like one uncertain. Then suddenly she swayed, as if about to faint. She grasped the door for support.

The lovers watched her in silence as eloquent as though they gazed upon a spirit. Then suddenly the man broke the spell of tense silence, and stooping to the andon raised it up and swung its light upon the woman's face.

A cry escaped his lips—a cry simultaneously echoed by the stranger. She stepped into the room, and with her hands behind her drew the sliding doors closed. Now against them she stood, looking about her with vague eyes.

"Who are you?" hoarsely sounded the voice of Junzo.

"Ask—her!" was the reply she made, indicating Sado-ko. Junzo slowly turned toward his fiancée. He saw her hands fall from her face, which in the dull light seemed now white as marble. She turned it toward the woman. Her voice was strange.

"I do not know you, lady," was her answer.

The one by the doors laughed with a fierce wildness, then threw her arms above her head with abandoned recklessness.

"You do not know me—you!" She laughed again. "You have reason to know me, Princess Sado-ko," she cried.

Cold and immovable still, the girl who but lately had clung so warmly to her lover, stared now upon the visitor.

"I do not know you," she repeated in distinct tones. "I am not a princess, lady, but a simple maiden, the daughter of Yamada Kwacho, and named Masago!"

Then, as though she put aside some late physical weakness, the other crossed and faced her.

"I am the maid Masago, with whom you exchanged your state, Princess Sado-ko," she said.

There was silence for a moment, then the low-toned, deliberate denial of the other one.

"It is not true," she said.

Masago turned toward the artist.

"Look at me!" she said. "You do not dare, you artist-man. You know that I speak truth."

As though she were an unholy thing, he shrank from her. She moved uncertainly about the room. Suddenly she asked quite querulously:—

"Where is my mother? I never realized before how much I loved her." She looked about the room impatiently. "How dark it is! Let us have light."

"No, no," cried out the artist, imploringly, "there is sufficient."

"Ah, you fear to see my face more plainly, artist? Yet I will have more light. My nerves are all unstrung. I could laugh and weep, and I could scream aloud at the least cause."

She clapped her hands loudly, imperiously, then restlessly paced the room.

"The woman always came so slowly. The promptness of the menials of Nijo makes me impatient of this country slowness."

Outside, in the corridors, the shuffling tread of the servant was heard. Masago, in her nervous state, could not wait for her to open the doors, but pushed them apart.

"Bring more lights," she commanded, then stayed the woman by grasping her kimono at the shoulder: "Oh, it is you I see, Okiku. Come inside!"

The woman stepped into the room, looking up at her in a startled fashion, then glancing at the other silent two.

"Do you recognize Masago?" asked the girl, bringing her face close to the servant's. The woman cried out in fright as she stared in horror from one to the other. Suddenly she gasped:—

"It is a wicked lie. You are not Masago. There is my sweet girl." She pointed to the silent Sado-ko.

At those words Sado-ko seemed to come to sudden life. She crossed the room and whispered to the maid:—

"Okiku, bid my father and my mother come at once. The woman seems both ill and witless. Pray hasten. Also bring more lights."

Masago sat down on the floor. Laying her head back against the panelling of the wall, she closed her eyes wearily.

"I am so tired and worn out," she said plaintively; "I have travelled half the night. What time is it, Onatsu-no—Why, I forget again. Oh, it is good to be home once more. I never knew how much—"

Ohano's pleasant voice was heard outside the door. As she bustled into the room, followed by Kwacho, Masago leaped to her feet, and, rushing headlong across the room, threw her arms about Ohano's neck.

"Mother! Oh, my mother, mother!" she cried.

Ohano stood in stiff amazement, staring across Masago's head at Sado-ko. The maid brought andons; the room was now well lighted.

"Why—what—" was all that Ohano could gasp, but she had not the heart to put the girl from her arms. Yamada Kwacho was more brusque, however. He drew the girl away from Ohano by her sleeves, but when he saw her face, he started in astonished bewilderment.

"I do not understand," he said dazedly, "Junzo—Masago—" He turned to them for enlightenment.

Sado-ko spoke with perfect clearness. Her eyes were wide and steady, but there was no color in her face.

"The woman seems demented, father. She thinks that she is other than herself—your daughter. But look upon her garments. See the crest upon her sleeves! She evidently is some high lady. Her mind is wandering in delusion."

With a savage cry Masago sprang toward her. She would have struck Sado-ko had not Kwacho held her.

"What! You—you speak thus in my own father's house! Oh!" She turned piteously toward Ohano. "Mother, you will understand. You know your Masago!"

"You, Masago!" exclaimed Yamada Kwacho; "why, you are wild in ways. Our girl from babyhood has been docile, quiet, almost dull, while you—"

"Mother, speak to me. Say that you at least know your own child."

Ohano burst into tears. Her mind was entangled and perplexed.

There were steps without the house, and the shrill calls of runners; then loud rappings on the doors. Kwacho pushed them open roughly to find a dozen men in livery upon his veranda. A tall man stepped forward. Sado-ko pulled her mother down with her upon the floor, thus concealing their faces in low obeisance. The artist did not move, but his eyes met those of the royal Prince Komatzu. The latter glared upon him fiercely.

"What means this rude intrusion?" demanded Kwacho. "We are simple citizens. Why are we disturbed?"

He was interrupted by the screaming of Masago. She rushed toward Komatzu, crying out:—

"You, you, you—He has sent *you* for me—oh-h—"

She swayed and fell even as she spoke.

Without a word of explanation the Prince Komatzu himself stooped to the floor. Lifting in his arms the senseless form of the maid Masago, he bore it to the royal norimon without the house.

After that those within the house heard the sounds of departure. Then silence in the night. Kwacho returned from the veranda.

"They have gone in the direction of the palace Aoyama—some demented princess, doubtless." He turned to Junzo, "I trust you will pardon the interruption of your visit in my house."

The artist returned his host's bow mechanically, then looked with some stealthiness toward his fiancée. When he found her eyes fixed upon his face imploringly, he could not look at her.

"The night grows late," he said heavily; "permit me to say good night."

He bowed deeply to all, departing without another word to Sado-ko. She moved toward the doors. Turning in the path, he saw her standing there.

That night, when husband and wife lay side by side upon their mattresses, Kwacho, moving restlessly, said:—

"The woman had a countenance so strangely like our girl's it disturbs my mind. Yet, Shaka! how different were their ways! How much more admirable the simple, unaffected manners of our country girl! I wonder why the woman came—"

"Listen, Kwacho," said Ohano, sitting up, "I have heard, sometime, that the Princess Sado-ko once loved our Junzo. Yes, it is so! You need not move so angrily. Do you not recall that when he was ill he called upon her name repeatedly?"

"I tell you," her husband answered angrily, "the boy is fairly sick with his affection for Masago. Only a woman's foolish mind could imagine otherwise."

Ohano lay down again.

"A woman's wiser mind, Kwacho. I am convinced this princess came to take our Junzo from Masago."

"Go to sleep, Ohano," growled her husband; "surmises and convictions are sometimes treasonable and wicked."

XXVII

A Gracious Princess at Last

The following morning Masago, irritated and nervous, sat in a chamber of the palace Aoyama. Impatiently she chided Madame Bara, the chaperon.

"I am tired of your voice," she said. "Do not speak further, or better still, leave me, if you please."

The woman, bowing deeply, left her mistress alone. Then Masago called:—

"Natsu-no! Where are you?"

Upon the instant appeared the waiting-woman of the Princess Sado-ko. Masago instructed:—

"Look out once again and tell me if he comes."

There was silence for a moment, as the maid passed into the adjoining room and leaning from the casement looked toward the front part of the palace. Soon her voice, raised and mechanical, answered the impatient query of Masago.

"He comes not yet!" she said.

"Look again," said Masago; "do not leave the casement until he comes."

Natsu-no was no longer young. She shivered at the open casement through which came the morning air; her eyes were blue with cold, and tired for sleep, for Natsu-no had spent the night in secret tears. After all these days she knew now where her mistress was, yet fate—a thing she was too insignificant to fight against—chained her like a slave to this girl-autocrat.

When, from the direction of the palace reserved for the men of the household, Komatzu appeared, the woman drew the shutters. Then, shuffling to the other room, she announced, "He comes!"

Masago sprang to her feet. She held out both her hands toward Komatzu when he entered, but he did not touch them. His eyes were dark, drawn into a heavy frown.

"Have you heard the joyful news?" she cried.

"What news?"

"Word came this morning by the divine barbarian wires from Tokyo that my betrothal with the Crown Prince had been peremptorily annulled. Why, you do not appear glad at the news!"

"I have heard it," he said; "there are other things which trouble me. Princess, I ask an explanation of your Highness. Nay, I demand it. Some months ago a rumor coupled your name with a low artist-man. You start and blush. Was the rumor only malice?"

Masago looked at him reproachfully. She said:—

"Purely so."

"Then, cousin, give me an explanation of your last night's conduct. You have recovered from your indisposition, which still had a cause. Why did you journey in such haste to Kamakura?"

Tears fell. Masago's voice broke and trembled. "I was homesick," she replied in a low voice; "that is the truth, Komatzu. The gods are my witnesses."

"Homesick for the merchant's home, friends of the artist-man?"

She averted her face, not hesitating in her deceit.

"Your jealousy is misplaced, Komatzu. They told you truly last night. I was—as women often are—witless. Who would not be at such a shock?"

"You speak of your betrothal?"

"I do. Do you not understand, Komatzu?"

She went closer to him. "The thought of union with another than yourself unnerved me."

He spoke impetuously, and as though a weight was lifted from his mind:—

"Princess, could I believe your words, I would be the happiest prince in all the land."

"Believe them," she pleaded. "It is the truth I speak; I swear it by all the eight million gods of heaven, and by our ancestor, the Sun-god. I went to Kamakura, rashly, blindly, wildly, because of love for you."

He looked searchingly into her eyes. Then as if satisfied he stooped and kissed her lips, a habit they had recently adopted at court.

"I have suffered, Sado-ko, more than I ever dreamed possible. I thought this artist-fellow was alone responsible for your action."

"Komatzu, he is already betrothed to the merchant's daughter, a simple maid, who bears a small resemblance to me."

He made a gesture of denial.

"That is impossible, princess. What, you compare one of her class with you! It is most gracious. No one in all the land can equal you in beauty."

She smiled in happiness.

"Your journey was a fortunate event, though a morsel for the gossips, princess. Do you know that this latest caprice so moved the young and easily shocked Crown Prince, that in disgust he hastened to his father, and on his knees besought him to grant another wife?"

They laughed.

"What happened next?"

"One hour after you left Tokyo, Sado-ko was humiliated, her betrothal being publicly annulled. It made a noisy story for a space."

"And next what happened?"

"Next, I too presented myself before his Majesty, who, being uncle as well as father, was ready to condone offence unfitted for a future Empress. Consequently, when I begged him to grant me your hand in marriage, he graciously consented."

"And you followed me at once?"

"At once."

When Komatzu had left her, Masago stood for some time looking from the casement of the palace.

"To think," she murmured, "of the folly I was near to committing but last night. The court is cold and heartless, yet it is my true, true home, for there is the only one on earth who loves me." She sighed. "I am an outcast from my childhood's home—even my stupid mother denies me. It was fitting!"

The voice of the waiting-woman, Natsu-no, broke upon her meditations.

"Exalted princess!" She turned slowly toward the woman. At her haggard aspect she was touched.

"What is it, Natsu-no?" she asked with compassion.

"I am no longer young," said the woman. "I was handmaiden to the mother of the Princess Sado-ko, and from her birth I served the latter."

"You have been faithful," said Masago, kindly.

"Will, then, the illustrious one reward the faithful service of the most humble one?"

"What do you wish? It is already granted," said Masago, generously, for she was happy.

"Permission," said the woman, "to leave your service."

Masago looked closely into her face.

"You wish to serve again—"

She did not finish the sentence, nor did the woman. Their eyes met. Each understood the other.

"You are free to go," said Masago, gently.

The woman moved away.

"Stay," said Masago, "I have a message for you to carry to your mistress. Say this for me: 'She who is now Princess Sado-ko sets free your maid. She wishes with all her heart she had done likewise with the nightingale.'"

Natsu-no touched with her head the hem of Masago's robe.

"You are a gracious princess," she murmured.

XXVIII

"The Gods Knew Best!"

It wanted but a few hours before the noon wedding when Sado-ko, appearing on her balcony, looked down into the garden, where her lover waited. Down the little flight of stairs straight to him she went, silently accepting from his hands flowers. Her eyes were fixed upon his face lovingly, but anxiously.

"You look so pale," she said. "Did you not sleep last night, my Junzo?"

"I did not sleep," he said. "Come, let us walk where it is more secluded. I wish to speak with you alone."

In a dreamy, pensive fashion she walked beside him. They crossed the little garden bridge to a quiet, shady spot. Once out of sight of the house, Junzo stopped short and, turning, faced her.

"Last night," he said, "one told a nightmare story, which you denied. The morning is come. Tell me the truth."

A flush spread over her face, as though she were half angered with him. She would not raise her eyes to his. His voice was firm—stern:—

"Answer me."

"I cannot," she replied, "when you speak in such a tone."

Her heaving bosom told him she was on the verge of tears. Gently he took her hands in his and held them. His voice was tenderness itself.

"Now tell me all," he said.

She tried to meet his eyes, but could not. Then she sought to draw her hands from his, while she averted her face.

"I would not speak of sad matters on my wedding-day. There is naught to tell." She added the last sentence with swift vehemence.

"There is much to tell," he said gravely. "I am your lover—soon your husband. Before that time, tell me the secret which rests between us now. If there is no truth in that woman, reassure my doubts."

"Can love and doubt exist together?"

"If you loved me, you would trust me," he replied gravely, ignoring her question.

She threw her head back with a swift, brave motion.

"Do you truly love me?"

"With all my heart."

"You love Sado-ko?"

He did not answer.

"Ah, how blind you have been," she said, "that Sado-ko could make you think she were other than herself. It was a strange test of your love, Junzo."

"Then it is true!" he said, making a movement of recoil from her.

"It is true that I am Sado-ko," she said.

He stared at her blankly. Then suddenly he covered his face with his hands and groaned.

"The gods have pity on us both!" he said.

"Why should the gods have pity?" asked the Princess Sado-ko. "They have already blessed us. We are happy, Junzo."

"Happy!" he repeated. "Guileless one, do you not see our happiness is so slight and dangerous a thing we cannot hold it?"

"But why may we not?"

"You are the Princess Sado-ko, and I—an artist-man."

"You are my Junzo," she replied, "and I am your Sado-ko. This we know, but it is a secret. The world will call me Masago, and once I am your wife—"

"Our union is impossible."

Pressing her hand to her breast, she gazed imploringly at him.

"It is not impossible," she said steadily. "You cannot now refuse to marry me. The gods have given us to each other. They did so from the first. We will be happy."

"There are others of whom we both must think," he cried.

"No, no," she said. "Upon this day we will not think of others."

"This is folly that we have been dreaming, O princess!"

He moved away from her for a time, pacing up and down with moody, bent head. He came back to her impetuously, and spoke accusingly, yet mournfully:—

"You did a cruel act last night. That poor girl came to her true home. You denied her, Sado-ko!"

"*You* reproach me for that!" she cried, her eyes flashing resentfully. "How can *you* say that to me, since it was for your sake I did deny her, and for hers too, though she had been most eager and well content to change her lot with mine at first. Yet last night I thought upon the consequences of her act and mine. I did not think of myself at all."

He did not interrupt her, and she continued in defence with impetuous swiftness.

ONOTO WATANNA

"Think on the matter but a little while, Junzo. Would you have loved this other one? No, in your face I read the answer. Do not speak it. Could I give her to you, then, in place of me? I am but a woman and cannot reason harshly, and so I thought last night with pity and tenderness of you."

"My Sado-ko!" he said.

"A little while ago," she said, "you called me Masago. How easily you change the name. First it was Sado-ko,—the sweetest, most peerless name on earth. Then it was Masago,—the purest, simplest name for maiden; and now—"

"I never loved you for your name," he said.

She laughed for the first time, and caught at his hand, pressing it against her face.

"Now you are my Junzo once again. We will not speak of these sad things."

"Sado-ko, we cannot but do so. Try and see the matter as it is. You are—"

"Masago—your betrothed. A little while and I will be—your wife!"

"It cannot be," he said sadly, "for you are not Masago. We must think of her besides ourselves. We cannot rob her of her rights."

"But it is to protect her that I must still be Masago. Why, think what would be the fate of a common citizen if she confessed that she had practised deceit upon the royal court! True, I was jointly guilty, but princesses do not have the punishment bestowed upon a simple citizen. Why, there is no doubt, if this were told, the maid Masago would be punished by the government so cruelly she would not have the strength to live. Is it not a crime of treason—"

Junzo held up a hand, for some one was coming toward them.

The woman who approached was bowed, but when she lifted her face, they saw the undried tears upon it. Sado-ko recognized at once Natsu-no. The latter came hastily toward her, dropped upon her knees, and hid her face in the folds of the girl's kimono.

"Do not kneel," said Sado-ko. "They will see you from the house. Stand up. Now tell me, why do you come here?"

"Sado-ko!"

"Hush! Do not call me by that name. Why are you here?"

"To offer my poor services again, sweet mistress."

"You have left the Nijo service?" inquired Sado-ko, swiftly.

"The gracious princess granted me my freedom, and so I came—"

Sado-ko put her arm about her old servant.

"Do not tremble so, good maid," she said, "but tell us in a breath all there is to know."

"She is to marry Prince Komatzu. All is well with her to-day. In her happiness she was generous and gracious; and so this morning granted me my freedom."

Sado-ko turned a beaming face toward her lover. For the first time he was smiling.

"Your coming is a happy omen, good maid," he said.

"Hark, listen!" said Sado-ko, her eyes gleaming. "They are calling me. They wish to put my wedding gown upon me. I must go. Natsu! Come and dress me for the last time in my maidenhood. Junzo! For but an hour's space, sayonara!"

"Sayonara," he repeated with deep emotion.

He watched her until he could not see her further. Then with sudden, swift, and buoyant step he followed the path she had taken, and entered the wedding house.

"The gods knew best!" he said.

A Note About the Author

Winnifred Eaton, (1875–1954) better known by her penname, Onoto Watanna was a Canadian author and screenwriter of Chinese-British ancestry. First published at the age of fourteen, Watanna worked a variety of jobs, each utilizing her talent for writing. She worked for newspapers while she wrote her novels, becoming known for her romantic fiction and short stories. Later, Watanna became involved in the world of theater and film. She wrote screenplays in New York, and founded the Little Theatre Movement, which aimed to produced artistic content independent of commercial standards. After her death in 1954, the Reeve Theater in Alberta, Canada was built in her honor.

A Note from the Publisher

Spanning many genres, from non-fiction essays to literature classics to children's books and lyric poetry, Mint Edition books showcase the master works of our time in a modern new package. The text is freshly typeset, is clean and easy to read, and features a new note about the author in each volume. Many books also include exclusive new introductory material. Every book boasts a striking new cover, which makes it as appropriate for collecting as it is for gift giving. Mint Edition books are only printed when a reader orders them, so natural resources are not wasted. We're proud that our books are never manufactured in excess and exist only in the exact quantity they need to be read and enjoyed.

bookfinity™

Discover more of your favorite classics with Bookfinity™.

- Track your reading with custom book lists.
- Get great book recommendations for your personalized Reader Type.
- Add reviews for your favorite books.
- AND MUCH MORE!

Visit **bookfinity.com** and take the fun Reader Type quiz to get started.

Enjoy our classic and modern companion pairings!

Printed in the USA
CPSIA information can be obtained
at www.ICGtesting.com
JSHW082354140824
68134JS00020B/2069